Praise for *A Stroke of the Pen*

"*A Stroke of the Pen* contains the last pieces of fiction we are likely to see from the comic genius who created Discworld. . . . We could certainly use more of Pratchett's humor and wisdom just now. How apropos that, due to a typographical error, the motto of the major Discworld newspaper is 'The Truth Will Make You Fret.' Of course, it's another universally acknowledged truth that if you read just one of Pratchett's books, you'll want to read everything he wrote. That now includes *A Stroke of the Pen*."
—Michael Dirda, *Washington Post*

"Funny, fantastical, and slyly smart." —*Mail on Sunday*

"A collection of twenty excellent, often laugh-out-loud early works. . . . Pratchett devotees will be moved and gratified by this unexpected gift and even casual readers will be utterly charmed."
—*Publishers Weekly* (starred review)

"Delightful. . . . The wit, wisdom, and intelligence are interspersed with a lively dose of naivete, with entertaining results."
—*The Independent* (London)

"Pratchett aficionados will find *A Stroke of the Pen* a treasure trove glittering with lost gems." — *Financial Times*

"These early stories show Pratchett's remarkable ability to poke fun at the absurdity of the real world through fantasy full of irreverent wordplay, silly authority figures, and subverted endings. . . . Pratchett's legion of fans will relish the view through this almost-overlooked window into the author's evolution." —*Booklist* (starred review)

"*A Stroke of the Pen* shows [Pratchett] at a stage when he was stopping at the first or second tree. Soon he would plunge into the forest."
—*Sunday Times*

"A short and slightly bittersweet portrait of Pratchett as a young writer. . . . [The stories] reflect an author in search of his craft. . . . The earliest seeds of what later became Discworld are there for readers who still miss his inimitable style." —*Library Journal*

Books by Terry Pratchett

A complete list of Terry Pratchett books can be found at www.TERRYPRATCHETT.COM.

A Stroke of the Pen

Pen

The Lost Stories

TERRY PRATCHETT

HARPER

NEW YORK • LONDON • TORONTO • SYDNEY

HARPER

Published in the U.K. in 2023 by Doubleday, an imprint of Transworld Publishers.

A hardcover edition of the book was published in 2023 by Harper, an imprint of Harper-Collins Publishers.

All interior illustrations copyright © 2023 by Andrew Davidson.

HarperCollins books may be purchased for educational, business, or sales promotional use. For information, please email the Special Markets Department at SPsales@harpercollins.com.

FIRST HARPER PAPERBACKS EDITION PUBLISHED 2024.

The Library of Congress has catalogued the hardcover edition of this book as follows:

Names: Pratchett, Terry, author.
Title: A stroke of the pen : the lost stories / Terry Pratchett.
Description: First edition. | New York : Harper, 2023.
Identifiers: LCCN 2023032374 (print) | LCCN 2023032375 (ebook) | ISBN 9780063376199 (hardcover) | ISBN 9780063376205 (paperback) | ISBN 9780063376212 (ebook)
Subjects: LCSH: Fantasy fiction, English. | LCGFT: Short stories.
Classification: LCC PR6066.R34 S776 2023 (print) | LCC PR6066.R34 (ebook) | DDC 823/.914--dc23/eng/20230804
LC record available at https://lccn.loc.gov/2023032374
LC ebook record available at https://lccn.loc.gov/2023032375

ISBN 978-0-06-337620-5 (pbk.)

24 25 26 27 28 LBC 5 4 3 2 1

This volume is dedicated to Pat and Jan Harkin who have spent countless hours in the British Newspaper Archive in Boston Spa, Yorkshire, establishing the dates when the episodes of the story "The Quest for the Keys" were actually published. As Rob Wilkins and I did not initially know when they appeared, Pat and Jan had to check through thousands of issues of the *Western Daily Press* and, while doing so, discovered stories written by Terry under the pseudonym Patrick Kearns, which are republished here for the first time.

And to Chris Lawrence who at the age of fifteen was so impressed with Terry's story "The Quest for the Keys" that he tore out the pages from the *Western Daily Press* in which it appeared and kept them for forty years before he cut out the columns, removing their dates, with happy consequences. Had he not done so, the Harkins would not have gone on their search and thus unearthed all the rest of the stories in this book.

We are deeply in their debt.

Colin Smythe

Contents

CONTENTS

Foreword by Neil Gaiman

Terry Pratchett being now these eight years dead, I have watched at first hand as the living person I knew has become a legend of sorts. Terry is, in the popular mind, as far as I can tell, a beaming, gentle, wise soul of twinkling eye and noble mien, a sensible old comforter, able to be enlisted by people of widely differing beliefs into their camps because of course their Terry would have agreed with them, they love his books, don't they? And I cannot help but feel that this semi-mythical Terry, like Merlin but with a witty quip instead of a wand and a slightly shorter beard, might as well exist in the popular mind as any other Terry Pratchett.

He is merrier than the Terry I remember, significantly less irascible, much less likely to hold opinions you disagree with (whoever you are reading this, whatever it is you believe, I promise that the real Terry held at least one opinion that would have made you curl your toes and go "Oh, come on, you don't really think that!"); he is levelheaded and always lovable. The real Terry Pratchett was certainly lovable, but not always. He had, as he would have been the first to tell you, his days. Even I, and I still miss the real person I remember, am occasionally grateful for the new revised semi-legendary Terry Pratchett: we rarely disagree about what's happening when I'm making *Good Omens*, for example, and that Terry mostly gives me his blessing to do as I think fit. (Having said that, we do disagree sometimes, or at least there are times when the Terry in my head is very clear on what we should be doing, and it's not what I would have wanted to do, and then I sigh and do what I'm pretty sure Terry would have wanted instead of doing what I would probably have done.)

Sometimes, when I think of Terry, I miss the bits of the stories Terry would tell me—or even show me—that were never published. They would have been, I am sure, on the hard disk that was crushed by a steamroller after his death. The fragment of the story about Rincewind's mother, for example. Or the Dunnikin Diver section of the novel *Moving Pictures*. They existed once but they are all gone now, crushed into fragments, bits and bytes reduced to bits and fragments of metal and silicon and glass.

When Rob Wilkins, Terry's representative on Earth, called me and told me that a trove of Terry Pratchett stories had been unearthed by brilliant and dogged detectorists hunting through newspaper archives, I was unsure what to think.

And then I read the stories. And I smiled.

I wondered, though, as I read them, what Terry would have thought of these stories being found and presented to the world. And then I realized, because people are complicated, even when they aren't being semi-legendary, it would probably depend which Terry, and at what point in his career.

The young Terry Pratchett who wrote them would have been proud of them, that's for certain. He's obviously working hard on them. He once told me that a journalist should think like a ram-raider—smash through the plate glass, grab what you can, and disappear into the night. These are ram-raider stories: he has a certain amount of space on the newspaper page, which means a certain number of words to fill it, no less and no more, and he's going to start, build and finish his story to the word count. He's going to hook you as quickly as he can and drag you through to the end.

He's not a humorist, not yet, and he's definitely not the blazing satirist he would become. The Terry Pratchett who wrote these stories is a journalist who thinks that he is, in his soul, a science fiction writer, even if that's not what he's currently writing. (He told me when we first met that he was a science fiction writer. I believed him.) This Terry is the man who has written *The Dark Side of the Sun* and *Strata*, mashing up his favorite tropes by Larry Niven and Isaac Asimov, determined in each book to build his own universe from scratch but as yet unsure what he will do with it.

The stories in this book are, on the other hand and for the most part, set in the here and now. Or at least the hereish and the nowish. And they are, also for the most part, funny and fantasies. They feel more like the precursors of Discworld (or even the world of *Good Omens*) than either of Terry's two early SF novels do.

It's one of the hardest parts of being a writer, the growing up in public bit. Terry needed to be published. He didn't have the time to spend polishing his skills in private. The Patrick Kearns identity allowed him to write fiction, to hone his craft, to discover, I suspect, what kind of thing he enjoyed making up and writing down. During these twenty tales he tries out a number of techniques—"How It All Began . . ." uses the Cave People as Us, Inventing Things, for example, which Terry had encountered in one of his favorite books, Roy Lewis's *The Evolution Man*, while the Blackbury stories utilize a particular British Humor Style I tend to attribute to Norman Hunter, creator of *Professor Branestawm*, that is knowing and accessible for children, but with raisins of wit tossed in for adults. And through all of these stories we watch young Terry Pratchett becoming Terry Pratchett. There will be familiar turns of phrase, familiar names, there will be many moments where we see the mind of the Terry Pratchett that was still to come at play.

When does a young writer become the writer you love? Certainly "The Quest for the Keys" is absolute proto-Discworld Pratchett, even if Morpork had not yet found its Ankh, and reading it made me feel the same way I do when an art scholar unearths an early version of a famous painting I'm familiar with and love. Change a couple of variables and "The Quest for the Keys" might have been the template for *The Color of Magic*.

I suspect that the Terry Pratchett of the middle years, building Discworld and honing his craft, would have been slightly embarrassed by the rediscovery of these stories. The Patrick Kearns stories would have been a distraction to him.

And Sir Terry Pratchett, the writer in his final years? What would he think about these stories being found and published?

I think he would have been happy that they were there to delight fans, and to intrigue the Pratchett scholars. (I don't think he was ever comfortable with the existence of the Pratchett scholars, mind.)

I think he would have been proud of the young journalist who wrote them, and that, when he reread them, he might even have chuckled, amused or inspired by something a younger him had written, hidden behind an impenetrable pseudonym and buried in the dusty archives of the *Western Daily Press* for, the young Terry was certain, ever and ever and ever.

Neil Gaiman, May 2023

Introduction by Colin Smythe

It had always puzzled me that Terry's inspiration for writing his *Bucks Free Press*–style short stories had dried up during parts of the 1970s.

Actually it had not: I just had not looked carefully enough. At the time of his writing *The Dark Side of the Sun*, *Strata*, and his first Discworld novel *The Color of Magic*, he was also writing short stories for the *Western Daily Press* pseudonymously, and later once more under his own name.

So we welcome "Patrick Kearns" to the Pratchett canon: we guessed that Patrick sounds close enough to Pratchett, and Kearns was his mother's maiden name. And who else would have used Gritshire, Blackbury, Even Moor, and the Ministry of Nuisances in their stories, or an academic institute whose name, the Blackbury Institute of Applied Nonsense, sounds suspiciously like something from the future Discworld's Unseen University? I suspect that honorable practice among newspaper staff prevented him from writing in two papers at the same time under his real name, as at that time he was an employee of the *Bath and West Evening Chronicle*. But they have the unique hallmarks of tales by Terry Pratchett.

If it had not been for Chris Lawrence, who had torn out the relevant pages of the *Western Daily Press*, we would not have known of Terry's 1984 story "The Quest for the Keys," before

January 2022. As Chris had not kept their publication dates, uber-fans Pat and Jan Harkin started going through the issues from the 1970s and the 1980s in the British Newspaper Archive in Boston Spa, Yorkshire, until they found them, and in the process also discovered the Kearns stories.

For all the years I was Terry's publisher and then agent he never ever gave me any help in finding his shorter writings—but as he wrote in his dedication to me in *Dragons at Crumbling Castle*, there were stories he had "carefully hidden away and very deliberately forgot all about." Just how true these words were, I had no idea. Maybe he really had forgotten about them. Certainly, neither Rob Wilkins nor I had ever heard of them.

It is with the greatest pleasure that we can at last share Terry's lost stories with you now.

Colin Smythe

How It All Began ...

R ight from the start some of the older cavemen were completely against the idea.

"It's unnatural," they said. "Anyway, where's it going to end?"

But the younger cavemen said: "That's progress, grandad. Pass us another log."

The thing was called "fire," and it was brought back to the cave by Og the inventor, who said he found it eating a tree. You had to keep it in a little cage of stones, he said. It kept you "warm," he said, which was the opposite of what you felt when the rain dripped into the cave at night.

Hal the chieftain was a bit puzzled and worried by it.

"Are you sure nothing will go wrong this time?" he asked. "It was bad enough when I was hit by one of your throwing sticks."

"Spears," corrected Og. "That was a design error, that was. This is foolproof. If you don't feed it with wood, it dies."

"Remarkable," said Hal.

That night, the cavemen sat round the new fire and ate cold

mammoth while giant creatures trundled and sneezed in the dark night outside. Og talked at length about the amazing possibilities of his invention. Hal just chewed his mammoth and watched the flames.

The fire bit him.

"Ouch!"

"You shouldn't touch it," said Og hurriedly. "It's snappish."

"I'm going to bed," said Hal huffily, and shuffled off sucking his finger.

One of the women was appointed to look after the fire and keep it fed while the men were hunting. Soon it was part of the cave way of life.

Then, one day, Og accidentally dropped a lump of wild pig into the fire and invented cookery. Cookery! Even Hal couldn't disagree with that! There were twenty-seven ways of cooking mammoth, to start with.

There were dodo-egg omelettes with snake sauce. There were great slabs of baked boar with honey gravy. And, of course, there were toadstool pies and deadly nightshade soup, which was unfortunate.

"You can't make an omelette without breaking eggs," said Og cheerfully. "We all make mistakes."

There was no stopping him after that. He drew with charcoal on the cave walls and invented Art. He managed to tame a wolf puppy and invented Dogs. But the trouble really started later.

Og invented . . . well, he *happened* to leave some grapes in a bowl of water, and when he remembered them, they had fermented. The wine tasted lovely. When everyone came home from hunting, they all tried it too. All except Hal. He was still down on the plains chasing a particularly fast giraffe.

He stopped when he smelled smoke. It was coming from the cave.

"!" he thought. "The fire's broken loose!"

Hal dropped his giraffe and ran. All round the cave the grass and trees were ablaze, and he grunted and swore as he crashed through the hot ash. Inside, the tribe were peacefully sleeping off the effects of Og's latest invention.

"Wake up!" screamed Hal. "You've let the fire escape!"

And it was growing fast. For miles around great flames were crackling through the grass. Animals fled. Birds flew squawking out of the smoke.

Half blinded by smoke, choking in the hot air, the tribe were led by Hal down to the river. They slopped down among the rushes and burst into tears.

Hal was white with fury as he turned to the miserable Og.

"Right," he growled. "That's it. I'm not standing for any more. I've had enough. Everything you do leads to trouble. I'm a patient apeman, but this time you've gone too far. Get out of the tribe."

Og slunk away through the reeds without a backward glance.

"Is that wise?" asked Ug, one of the oldest apemen. "He'll perish all by himself."

Hal snorted.

"What chance has he left us, then? There'll be no game for miles around. The fire doesn't seem to have spread so far downriver. Come on. If we don't move on, we'll starve."

All the next day they trudged through the mud. Here and

there the fire was still burning, and where there were no flames there was just grey, hot ash.

In the evening it rained. The tribe slept fitfully in the branches of a charred tree, while growling sabre-toothed tigers prowled beneath them.

The rain continued all the next day. The tribe spent most of it huddled together in a little hollow in the rocks.

After a while someone said: "The fire was warm."

And someone else added: "Cooked zebra was one of the best things that ever happened to me."

As the sun sank into a mass of black clouds even Ug said wistfully: "He wasn't a bad sort, in his way."

Hal shivered. "He'd have probably set fire to the whole world if we'd let him," he muttered.

A wolf howled in the distance. Another one answered. It was much nearer.

Suddenly Hal saw the black shape padding around the edge of the hollow, and his hair stood on end.

Women and children in the center!" he yelled, reaching for a stone.

The wolves closed in. The apemen hit them with sticks and threw stones, but the wolves were desperate with hunger because of the fire. And more of them seemed to be appearing.

Then Og leapt into the hollow, holding a blazing branch in his hand. He hurled it at the wolves and started fiddling with an oddly shaped piece of wood. It was a bow. Arrows started raining down on the yelping pack.

He didn't say anything. When the last of the wolves had fled, he simply beckoned the tribe to follow him and led them to a small clearing where several zebras were roasting over a fire. Under some trees he had built a strange sort of cave out of branches and bracken. It looked warm and inviting.

Well, Hal couldn't refuse to let Og back into the tribe. Not since most of the apemen were already tucking in to slices of zebra.

"I followed you. I thought you might need me eventually," was all Og said.

Soon a little village had been built.

Og discovered that seeds would grow, and invented Farming.

He invented animal traps, which was a much better way of catching meat than hunting. Then he invented wings, and unfortunately decided to try them out from the top of a cliff.

But several up-and-coming young apemen had got the idea and they invented Civilization – eventually.

The village grew. Some of the open plain was turned into fields. Pretty soon hunters like Hal were beginning to look a bit foolish. That's how it all began.

Hal sat in front of his hut, looking thoughtful and feeling slightly uneasy.

"I wonder where it's all going to end?"

The Fossil Beach

D id you know that if you hold a seashell to your ear, you can hear the sea?

The noise gets stuck in the complicated curves of the shell and echoes around for ages. But what happens if it's a fossilized seashell? I'll tell you.

It so happened that in Gritshire, in the little seaside town of Shingle Regis, there was a tiny museum stuck on the end of the pier. It was really for the tourists, and was full of things like genuine mermaids' earrings, famous lifebelts, full-rigged ships in bottles,* and other rare and curious objects washed up by the sea.

The museum was run by a young man called Horace Breezeforth. One day he was in the museum counting the bubbles on a piece of unusual seaweed when a young woman came in and plonked a large fossil on his desk.

"Well, well, well," he said. "It's a genuine example of the extinct Rotundus snail. We could do with one of those."

---

* Actually built by very, very small boatbuilders, but that's another story.

The woman said her name was Jane Throckmorton and she was a geology student at Blackbury University.

"I found this in the cliffs down the coast," she said. "It's jolly interesting—you can hear the sea if you put it to your ear!"

And Horace could. But it wasn't the sea today—it sounded like the sea must have sounded millions of years ago. There was something very strange about it. And he could hear reptilian squawks and grunts, such as dinosaurs might make while paddling. He gasped in amazement.

"You wait," said Jane grimly. "You just listen!"

And Horace heard someone singing. It was a cheerful voice only just heard above the sound of the surf. It sounded familiar.

It went: "OOOOOO, IIIIII do like to be beside the seaside, O I do like to be beside the sea."

"That's impossible," cried Horace, almost dropping the shell. "There wasn't anyone alive in those days. Will you show me where you found this?"

Half an hour later, he and Jane scrambled down into a quiet rocky inlet just north of the town, and Horace saw the hole where she had chipped the shell out with her special geology hammer. There were quite a few fossils in the rocks.

"I'm jolly well going to get to the bottom of this," he muttered, picking up a spare hammer and striding towards the rocks.

They'd worked away for twenty minutes or so, when Horace began to uncover what looked like the bones of some very odd creature. After a while he realized what it was. It was a fossilized deckchair.

And Jane had started to unearth the remains of a small lizard. She dropped her hammer.

"Oh, those fossils are quite common round here," said Horace airily.

"Only this one's got a newspaper in its mouth," mumbled Jane. She held it out.

It was of course quite flat and had been turned into a sort of slate. But it was still just about readable.

Horace read out loud: "*The Blackbury Chronicle and West Gritshire Times.* I can't quite make out the date. Oh, yes, I—oh. Oh dear. It's today's."

Before long the beach was crowded. Policemen put up big screens round the rocks, and behind them Horace, Jane and several important men from Blackbury University were examining the fossils.

They were not really convinced until one of them happened to chip away a piece of a stone and found . . . a fossilized radio. It had been squashed flat by the tons of rocks on top of it over millions of years, but it was a radio all right.

"Well," said Horace. "Either dinosaurs were a lot brighter than we thought or something very strange has been going on."

"Do you know what I think?" said Jane. "I think there must be someone round here with a time machine who spends his holidays in the past, and is rather careless."

They left the professors examining the strange fossils and wandered up the cliff path to the heathery fields above. It was very hot, but there was a nice cool breeze off the sea. There was only one house to be seen. It was an old fisherman's cottage, snuggled down behind a couple of trees that had been so bent by the wind they were almost flat. There was a little garden full of fuchsias and cabbages, and in a little paddock at one side a goat tethered to a pole had eaten a big circle in the grass. There were a couple of beehives too.

"Who lives there?" asked Jane.

"An old boy called Dr. Golightly," said Horace. "He's the world's foremost lepip—lepida—He is very good at collecting butterflies.'

"Ugh," said Jane. "I don't like that. I always feel sorry for the poor things."

"I understand he keeps them alive in a sort of big cage and breeds them," said Horace. And as they walked past, they could see several giant wire-netting cages at the back of the house.

Just then, a butterfly shot past. It was blue and green, with gorgeous yellow specks.

And it was slightly larger than an eagle.

A moment later a small fat man came pounding through the bushes, waving an enormous butterfly net. He was dressed in a big sunhat, a pair of faded shorts, and had a long white beard.

"I say, did you see a Golightlius giganti go past?" he panted.

"It flew out to sea," said Horace. "That's if you mean that big butterfly?"

"Call that big?" said the old man. "Goodness, it's just a baby—er, excuse me. I'd better be getting back." He disappeared into the bushes again.

There was a long pause. "That was Dr. Golightly," Horace said.

"But butterflies like that don't exist!" shouted Jane.

"They used to," said Horace thoughtfully. "Millions of years ago insects sometimes grew to be very big, you know."

They both thought about the odd fossils, and the seashell which sang "I Do Like to be Beside the Seaside" . . .

Five minutes later they were knocking at the cottage door, but there was no reply. But in the cages round the back Horace saw several enormous butterflies. One or two were so big they had perches, like birds.

They came back next day. There was still a lot of activity going on down at the beach. One of the professors had found what looked like a fossilized fishing net.

Horace knocked at the cottage door again, and then found it was open. Feeling a bit burglarous they went inside. It was quite dark. An old clock ticked slowly in the corner, and the room was full of rather shabby but comfortable-looking furniture.

And there was a strange buzzing noise. It seemed to be coming from a little cupboard under the stairs. Horace opened it.

He found that he was looking out on a beach. Big ferns grew here and there, and the cliffs towered away in the distance. The sun looked big and yellow. He closed the door quickly and it looked just like an ordinary cupboard. He opened it again, and there was the beach.

"Right, then," he said bravely, and stepped through. After a moment's hesitation, Jane followed him, and they stood side by side on the sand. Behind them, hovering just above the ground, was a sort of picture of the inside of the cottage.

"I've got a feeling we've just stepped millions of years into the past," said Horace. He pointed upwards. Several large butterflies skimmed over the ferns.

"I wonder how he does it?" said Jane. "I mean, the cottage didn't even have electricity."

Horace rolled a large boulder across the sand and wedged it in the opening.

"I hope that'll do," he said. "I want to make sure we can go back again. I don't fancy being fossilized."

They wandered along the beach. Occasionally some giant lizards glided overhead on leathery wings, and once they saw what Jane said was a brontosaurus. It was eating ferns, a haystack-full at a time, but stopped to peer down at them. It was about the size of a house.

"They're quite harmless," said Jane, patting it on the snout. "They're vegetarians. Do you know that they're so big that if you trod on its foot, it wouldn't realize it for two days?"

"Er, no," said Horace.

They broke through a fern thicket and almost fell over Dr. Golightly. He was sitting in a deckchair, shaking his portable radio.

"Damn thing won't go," he said. "All it picks up is a lot of nothing."

"I shouldn't think they had a BBC in these days, unless it was the Brontosaurus Bellowing Contest," said Horace.

"Oh, hello," said the doctor, peering at them. "Strange. Didn't I see you the other day? What are you doing back here in the Jurassic? Would you like a cup of tea?"

The doctor was brewing tea over a camping stove. They were all very thirsty and while they sat down in the fern thicket Horace told the doctor about how they found the strange cupboard under the stairs.

"It happens every second Tuesday," said the doctor. "Blessed if I know why."

"Do you come here often, then?" asked Jane.

"Oh yes. It's very handy. There are some splendid butterflies, you know, and of course there's absolutely no one else around. There won't be for millions of years."

"We heard you singing 'I Do Like to be Beside the Seaside,'" said Horace. "In a shell."

"My dear fellow, do I look the sort of person to sing comic songs? It must have been someone else."

Jane said: "Gosh, just think, there could be people having their holidays all through prehistoric times! How do you get back?"

Dr. Golightly held up a large alarm clock. "The gateway closes after seven hours," he said. "That's why I keep this clock by me."

Horace looked at it, and then at his watch.

"The sand's got at it," he said. "It's been stopped for two hours!"

Five minutes later they scrambled through the ferns just in time to see the glowing hole disappear. The rock Horace had wedged in it was cut in half.

There was a long, dreadful pause. Then Dr. Golightly said: "Oh. Well. At least the weather here is always nice. And I daresay we can live on shellfish for a fortnight."

They spent a very uncomfortable night on top of a rock while strange creatures grunted and sneezed in the undergrowth. Jane had a bit of a cry, and decided that wasn't much good, so she wondered how you cooked shellfish instead.

It was a lot better in the morning. They got a fire going by focusing sunlight through Dr. Golightly's thick glasses and made a sort of mussel stew in the teapot.

"This isn't half bad," said Horace admiringly, and after breakfast he paddled off catching prehistoric fish in the doctor's butterfly net. It was a lot better than sitting in the stuffy museum all day, and after a while he started singing. He stopped suddenly when he saw a large empty shell lying near him on the beach.

"So, it was me we heard!" he thought. "No wonder the voice sounded familiar! That's the shell we found fossilized!"

He ran back up the shore to find the others. They had decided to explore along the coast, and he caught sight of them just as they were rounding a heap of rocks.

When he caught up with them, they were looking down into a small bay backed by low cliffs.

"The sun's very hot," said Dr. Golightly. "I think we must be seeing things. This is undoubtedly millions of years ago, isn't it? Well, look down there."

Nestling against the cliff was a small, thatched house with roses round the door, and a neat lawn in front of it—though the effect was rather spoilt by a small dinosaur who was tethered with a piece of string and was eating the roses. A sign hung outside the door.

It said: THE OLD RED SANDSTONE LION.

"It's a pub," said Horace.

They scrambled across the rocks towards it, and it didn't disappear.

Inside, it was rather gloomy. There was a dartboard, and horse brasses hung on the walls. A long line of tankards hung from a beam, and, despite the hot weather, there was a fire in the grate. A small lizard was snoring in front of it.

A door opened behind the bar and a small bald man stepped out. He was wearing a big smile and a bright red waistcoat.

"Good morning!" he said, in a squeaky voice. "Lovely day! When are you from?"

"When?" said Horace. "1973, I suppose."

The little man looked at them in amazement.

"That's very early! We don't often get people from the twentieth century—not that I'm saying anything against it, mind," he added diplomatically.

Horace ordered a large lemonade all round and decided to tell the man—whose name was Mr. Buncombe—all about their adventure. He listened carefully.

"What you got there is what we call a side effect," he said at last. "The Temporal Express passes through on a Tuesday. It can cause these openings."

"What is the Temporal Express?" asked Jane.

It turned out that it was a big time machine which traveled regularly between the twenty-fifth century and various prehistoric times. They heard that in the twenty-fifth century it was quite the thing to take your holidays in the past. That was why Mr. Buncombe had built The Old Red Sandstone Lion.

"We get a very good class of people here," he said. "This is the offseason. I don't say anything against the Triassic and Carboniferous Ages, though. They're all right if you like hot steamy weather."

"Carboniferous?" said Horace, bewildered.

"That was when coal was laid down," said Jane. "Didn't you learn anything at school? It was millions of years ago."

Mr. Buncombe pointed to a large poster on the wall. It

showed a giant dragonfly whizzing through a swampy jungle and said: "Come and See Coal Made! Hunt the Giant Dragonflies in the Sultry Carboniferous!" At the bottom, in smaller lettering, it said: "Issued by Pre-Cambrian Timeways Ltd. Registered Office: AD 2455."

Mr. Buncombe looked at them thoughtfully.

"There might be trouble," he said. "You see, people from the twentieth century are not really supposed to know about this. I'm not sure the Time Police will let you go back. It might cause issues."

"But there's the fossilized newspaper," began Horace.

"Oh, people will soon think that's a trick of some sort," said Mr. Buncombe. "Excuse me."

He picked up what looked like a very complicated telephone and dialed a long series of numbers. Then he held a mumbled conversation with someone.

"That was time headquarters in 2500," he said. "I told them about you, and they're stopping the Temporal Express especially for you. This is only a request stop, you see. They say you can go back but you'll have to let them hypnotize you into forgetting all about this, or there might be trouble."

"Er," said Dr. Golightly. "Would anyone object if I stayed here? It's a nice place. I like it better than the twentieth century. Think of the butterfly collection I could make!"

"Well, we could do with a relief barman," said Mr. Buncombe. "I'd be glad of a little company."

"I'd like to get back to the twentieth century," said Horace. "It's not much, perhaps, but it is my home."

"And me," said Jane.

There was a kind of squashed bang outside the pub and a long silver cylinder materialized in the air. The door in its side slid back and someone said: "Jurassic! Jurassic! Next stop the Old Stone Age and all stations to 2700!"

Jane and Horace said goodbye to Dr. Golightly and climbed aboard.

There was a blue flash, and they woke up sitting on the cliffs overlooking the sea. Down below was the familiar outline of the pier, and there were yachts in the bay.

"Mmm," said Horace. "I feel a bit dizzy."

"I know what you mean," said Jane. "I'm sure there was something I ought to remember. Have you ever heard of a pub called the—the—er, I don't remember."

"Let's try and remember over lunch," said Horace, helping her up.

A couple of months later, Horace and Jane got married and settled down to live happily ever after. Although there was something that did puzzle them. Someone sent them a post-card. It must have been trick photography, because it showed several dinosaurs, grazing. The stamp was odd, too—it was a big "T" on a blue background, and was postmarked "Jurassic Post Office."

The postcard said: "Having a lovely time. Weather forecasters say it'll be fine here for the next two million years. Wish you were here."

And they never did find out who sent it.

The Real Wild West

This is a story of the real wild west.

It was sheep rodeo time in the little English-Welsh border town of Llanoggie, and the streets were full of sheep, big hairy sheep farmers and small, shifty-looking, black and white dogs.

The town's two pubs—the Three Feathers, on the Welsh side of the street, and the Hearts of Oak on the other—were doing a roaring trade and several windows had already been broken.

Things were even rowdier than usual because the Great Coal Rush of 1871 was in full swing, and the town was packed with grizzled coal prospectors, who had come in to stake their claims. And also to claim their steaks, since it was dinner time.

Pianos were playing, dogs were barking, fights were breaking out and the town was settling down to make a red-hot night of it.

So noisy was it that Mr. Owen Jones, half asleep in the back room of the Llanoggie Post Office, Telegraph Office, and Sweet Shop, almost missed the morse code message that came clicking along the wires from distant Hereford.

"Good heavens!" he cried, as he listened to the dots and dashes. Snatching a pencil, he hurriedly wrote down the message and limped over to the Three Feathers.

The public bar was full of smoke.

"Is Big Dai here?" shouted Mr. Jones.

A giant of a man with a great black beard looked up from where he was playing a rough and tough game of dominoes with a gambler from Cardiff.

"Look at this, Big Dai!" said Mr. Jones.

Big Dai read the message. It said: PC MCDOUGAL ARRIVES TONIGHT LLANOGGIE STOP FAR TOO MUCH LAWLESSNESS GOING ON STOP THIS MUST STOP STOP CHIEF CONSTABLE HEREFORD.

Big Dai, the biggest sheep-rustler, leek-runner, and pony thief in the border country, laughed so much he fell off his chair. A few dominoes slid out of his sleeve.

Soon everyone was laughing (it was safest to laugh when Big Dai laughed).

"If we don't send him packing inside a week, Llanoggie isn't the town I thought it was, boyo," he said, "and I'll have his helmet hanging up over my mantelpiece too!"

An hour later a figure in blue pedaled his regulation police bike down the High Street.

"He doesn't look very tall in the saddle," said Big Dai, who was leaning against the wall outside the Feathers.

"Just out of nappies, look you," said Dylan Morgan, who was known and feared everywhere as the Lone Crofter.

PC Hamish McDougal, late of Hendon Police College, carefully leant his bike against the wall of the old police station.

There had been several previous attempts to bring law and

order to Llanoggie, but Big Dai and the rest had put a stop to that.

There was dust everywhere in the police station. It was also full of sheep. A very small and tatty man in a large hat and virulent whiskers was asleep in a cell.

"Hey—" began Hamish. Something sank its teeth into his thick serge trousers. He could feel the fangs holding his leg in a vicelike grip.

"Eh? Oh, it's the police. Heh, heh, heh! All right, Sandy, let go. She's apt to be a mite hasty with strangers," said the whiskered man.

Hamish dared to look down, and saw a large, moth-eaten sheepdog release its grip and crawl away under the cell bunk.

The whiskered man stood up and shook his hand.

"Who are you?" asked Hamish.

"They call me Crabapple Evans. I'm by way o' being caretaker here, ever since the last policeman left."

"All right," said Hamish, sitting down on a dusty bench. "Tell me about Llanoggie."

"A terrible place, boyo, a terrible place. Daffodil smuggling, poaching, and fights up at the coal mines every night. They've got through twenty-seven policemen in the last year. Heh, heh!"

Crabapple unhooked a large Welsh harp from a nail on the wall.

"Excuse me, time for my evening practice," he said. "I'm training for the Llanoggie Bardic Contest. If I was you, I'd go over to the Three Feathers and introduce yourself. Heh, heh!"

As Hamish proceeded along the High Street, he heard Crabapple's twangy voice coming through the cell window. It sang:

"Do not forsake me, Blodwen Morgan,
On this our wedding day . . ."

Inside the Three Feathers, the hands of the clock pointed to ten past nine, as they had done for the previous fifteen years. It was in fact five minutes past closing time.

Big Dai and the Lone Crofter were playing darts against a couple of city slickers from Hereford, and winning by means of cunningly weighted darts. Was there no underhand business Big Dai would not stoop to?

The Lone Crofter hummed a little tune and then hissed: "I did hear the London coal train will be coming through Llanoggie tomorrow night, loaded with best coal and the mine owners' savings in gold."

"Did you now, boyo?" said Big Dai, thoughtfully. "Shame if it got accidentally robbed, wouldn't it be? I shall have to think about this."

Just then PC McDougal appeared in the doorway. He said in a regulation voice (a bit uncertainly because this was his first official duty):

"Evenin' all. Hullo, hullo, hullo, what's all this then? Ten forty-five and not closed yet?"

The barman shrugged, as if to say that the pub never closed until Big Dai said so. Everyone was waiting to see just what Big Dai would do.

But instead of losing his temper, he bowed and said: "I do believe this gentleman is right. Come along now, lads, drink up, we mustn't break the law on any account."

"Er—well, just see it doesn't happen again," said Hamish, rather pleased with himself.

"Why didn't you bop him one?" said the Lone Crofter as they left the pub.

"We don't want to arouse any suspicions if we're going to rob the express tomorrow," said Dai. "Leave him till afterwards. Round up the gang and we'll lay plans."

Now it so happened that late the following afternoon Crabapple was up near the deep cutting where the main railway line passed by Llanoggie, catching rabbits. He was moving softly and staying under cover, because the rabbits didn't belong to him, and the land wasn't his anyway. He heard voices and, peering through the bushes, he saw Big Dai and his men. They were piling sleepers across the track!

And just a few inches away from Crabapple stood the Lone Crofter . . .

A twig cracked under Crabapple's hand.

"Who's that?" cried the Lone Crofter, spinning round.

"There's no one here but us rabbits," said Crabapple, and suddenly wished he hadn't. Next moment he was bounding away for dear life.

The Lone Crofter plunged after him but at that moment Sandy, Crabapple's dog, leapt through the bushes and bit his leg.

"****!!" swore the Lone Crofter.

PC McDougal was just sitting down when Crabapple burst in. "They—they—they—" panted the old man.

"They what?"

"They're going to derail the express!"

"What?!" Hamish jumped up and grabbed his helmet. They dashed out to his bicycle—and found that both wheels had been removed.

"Big Dai is up at the cutting now!" said Crabapple.

Hamish glanced at the town clock. "The train will be coming through in a few minutes," he said. "Quick: is there anyone else around here who owns a bicycle?"

"Well, I've got an old one in the shed round the back," began Crabapple.

And it really was old, a penny-farthing with solid rubber tires. They wobbled off down the street, with Crabapple pedaling furiously and PC McDougal hanging on to his belt, while the dog Sandy ran barking along behind.

"I know where we can stop the train before it gets to the cutting," said Crabapple, as they sped along. "Only trouble is, there's a rather steep hill . . ."

They heard the train whistle as they topped the rise and there below them they could see the express winding through the valley. Crabapple freewheeled downhill.

Trees and bushes rushed by. Sandy was left a long way behind. The bike wheels were spinning so fast they were invisible.

"Can you put the brakes on?" shouted Hamish, above the rushing wind.

"What are brakes?" shrieked Crabapple.

Smoke started to pour out of the bearings, and the wheels' axles were beginning to glow red hot.

In a first-class carriage in the express, Sir Humphrey Clinker, mine owner, was reading *The Times* when his eye was caught by a very unusual sight.

An old-fashioned bicycle was drawing level with the speeding train. Steering it was a bewhiskered old man singing "Land of My Fathers" at the top of his voice. A young policeman was hanging on to the saddle and trying, with his helmet, to beat out the flames that were crackling over the wheels.

"How curious," said Sir Humphrey.

The policeman looked up and seemed to make up his mind. With one bound he leapt from the bike and clung to the side of the swaying carriage.

He scrambled in through the open window and shouted: "Where's the communication cord, in the name of the law?"

"My dear sir, you mustn't pull the communication cord unless it's an emergency," said Sir Humphrey. "There's a fine of five pounds if you do, you know."

"This is an emergency!" cried Hamish.

Sir Humphrey stood up and reached for the cord. "In that case, my dear sir," he said, "allow me to indulge a boyhood ambition."

His hand gave a quick downward jerk. Every wheel on the train locked solid. The express came to a juddering halt a few yards before Big Dai's barricade.

"My word," said Sir Humphrey. "If I'd known it was this enjoyable, I'd have jolly well risked five pounds before now."

Hamish raced up the train and caught Big Dai, who was scrambling into the guard's van. But the Lone Crofter and the rest of the gang were there too.

"Tie him up!" snarled Big Dai.

But his men were staring in horror at something behind him. Tearing along the side of the track came a great cloud of black smoke and red flames, in the middle of which could be dimly seen a smoke-stained face making strange noises.

Next moment Crabapple was upon them. His bike hit a rock, exploded, and filled the air with sparks and bits of metal.

Hamish seized his chance and caught Big Dai in the Hendon Police College No. 24 (b) Regulation judo hold.

Crash! went a wheel, landing on the Lone Crofter's head.

PC McDougal said: "I have reason to believe"—

Thud! went Crabapple, dropping out of the sky and onto several of the robbers.

—"that you can help me"—

Snarl! went Sandy, as her jaws tripped up another robber.

—"with my inquiries," finished PC McDougal.

He and Crabapple, who was appointed Acting Temporary Special Constable, lined up the stunned gang, handcuffed them together, and marched them to Llanoggie jail.

Things were very quiet in the town that night.

Hamish stood at the door of the police station and listened to Crabapple singing a new song: "Hang Down Your Head, Big Dai."

"Yep, I reckon it's going to be peaceful in Llanoggie from now on," said Hamish.

And it was, for about three days. Llanoggie was a very tough town.

How Scrooge Saw the Spectral Light (Ho! Ho! Ho!) and Went Happily Back to Humbug

"Ooh. Oooooooooh!" said Marley's ghost unconvincingly, rattling his chains.

Scrooge peered blearily into the gloom.

"Wassat?" he said, pulling the bedclothes around him.

"Ooooh, Ebenezer Scrooge, it is I, Marley, your old friend and business partner what accidentally fell off the top of a twelve-story building, ahem," said the ghost.

It was hung with spectral chains, and shackled to one ghostly ankle was an ancient luminous IBM 1456 adding machine.

Marley went on: "Anyway, what I mean is, I bin sent to show you the error of your ways . . . cor, this isn't a bad place at all, Ebenezer, you done all right for yourself!"

Scrooge had switched on the light. His bedroom walls were hung with very expensive silk and the bedcover was made of ermine. Instead of the traditional nightshirt and cap with a bobble on it, Scrooge was wearing James Bond kung-fu pyjamas.

"Oh, so it's you, my old business colleague Marley, what fell off the top of a twelve-story building before I could stop him, ahem ahem," said Scrooge. "How's things in the ghost biz?"

Marley looked a bit surprised. "Oh, you know, not so good, not so bad," he muttered.

Scrooge slipped out of bed into a gold-embroidered dressing gown.

"Look here, old chap, what's this all about? This is the second time you've come a-haunting of me. Remember? Clank, clank, you went. I don't mind telling you, you made a big impression on me. Clank, clank. A big impression. Better man for it, and all that. Mr Dickens made a big point about it all."

"Yes, but—" began Marley's ghost.

"I used to hate Christmas," said Scrooge, opening a cocktail cabinet. "Whiskey, or don't you touch spirits? Haha. Anyway, all that's behind me. Oh yes, you made me see the error of my ways—"

"I give up," muttered the ghost, and gave a shrill whistle.

There was a pop, and a second spirit manifested in the middle of the room. It had short curly hair, a big smile, carried a shimmering book in one hand and appeared to be speaking into a microphone.

"Arrgh," shrieked Scrooge. "It's the Eamonn O'Fizzy!"

"Yes, Ebenezer," crooned the spirit. "Do you remember this voice? Begorrah!"

"Yes, that's your voice," mumbled Scrooge, unimpressed.

"I meant this voice!" snapped O'Fizzy.

"God bless us every one," said a tiny little voice.

Scrooge gasped theatrically.

"It is! It isn't! Gosh! It is!" he cried. "It's Tiny Tim."

"Begot. Yes, Scrooge. And now we go back . . ."

And as if on a ghostly telly, Scrooge saw the scene in the Cratchit household, with all the family sitting happily round the table.

"Yes, that's the Cratchit family all sitting happily round their household table after I mended my ways and became a better person and decided to like Christmas."

"And then you bought up cracker companies, and turkey farms, and paper chain foundries, and polystyrene snowmen factories . . ."

"That's right. And spray-on snow shops, a balloon factory and a factory that made plastic Father Christmases for nasty little cakes with pink icing," said Scrooge. "And I merged them all together until I had one big Christmas company . . . UniScrooge!"

Then, O'Fizzy disappeared, but there was a fountain of colored lights and a second horrible vision bounced in. It was terrible; Scrooge clutched at the curtains.

"It's . . . It's . . ." he gibbered, staring at the huge chin that leered over him.

"You all right, dear?" said the Bruce Forsooth. "I'm here to take up the story as of now. All right?"

Scrooge saw a vision of shops filled with UniScrooge products. There were hard little lumps of soap in reams of Christmas wrapping that must have been very valuable, since it sent the price of the soap up one thousand per cent.

There were huge hot stores filled with swearing dads, screaming kids and normally nice mums shouting, "Just you wait till I get you 'ome and I won't 'arf give you what for!"

There were boxes of 2p crackers at 45p a cracker, each one with a genuine lump of plastic in it.

There were dry cigars and cheery corkscrews and people getting drunk at parties and driving cars into each other.

There were telly programs like *One Thousand Old Clips of Walt Disney's Films You've Already Seen Ten Times.*

The vision fogged for a moment, and then showed the very fat and fed-up Cratchit family lying groaning around their twenty-seven-inch color TV. They didn't seem all that happy.

On the screen a bunch of blasphemous atheists in paper hats were trying to whip up some sort of enthusiasm for the Christmas Spirit in a studio full of cold lights.

"Remember the old days, Mrs. C?" said Bob Cratchit. "We enjoyed ourselves then. I've just about had a bellyful of Christmas this year . . . never again!"

The vision and Bruce Forsooth disappeared, only to be replaced by a truly terrible thing with rolling eyes and a twisted grin that had Scrooge shrieking with terror.

"No, not the Hugey Grin!" he screamed.

"Thank you, thank you, friends," said the apparition. "And let's have a big hand for the Bruce Forsooth there, didn't he do well? And now, friends, this is what Christmas Future has in store . . ."

There was a brief vision of darkened shops and gloomy streets before the scene faded out because of embarrassment.

". . . What happened?" said Scrooge.

"Everyone said never again," said the Hugey Grin.

"No more Christmas?" mumbled Scrooge.

"'They didn't see the point," said the Hugey Grin. "You can have too much of a good thing."

Scrooge woke up the next morning and immediately went to the window. He looked at the jolly street lights the shopkeepers had put up to save themselves from having to be polite to the customers.

He also saw a tough-looking little boy.

He'd sell all his Christmas factories. He'd sell his television studios. He'd go back to being a miser, which was at least healthy.

That would have to wait. But he could make a start in a small way right now.

"Hey," he shouted to the boy. "Here's a fiver. There's another one waiting for you if you go round to the Cratchits' and kick their telly in."

Then he shut the window.

"Humbug," he thought cheerfully. "Humbug."

Wanted: A Fat, Jolly Man with a Red Woolly Hat

"**I**'ve quit," said Father Christmas. He flicked his red cap onto the hook behind the door and nudged the cat out of his armchair.

Mrs. Christmas stood in the kitchen doorway, furiously beating a Yorkshire pudding mixture.

"Ho, yes," she said sharply. "What brought this on, may I ask?"

"I was checking the presents list and I thought, blow this for a lark. I've been doing this for five hundred years and what've I got to show for it? No prospects, no pension. Ho! Ho! Ho! I thought, time for a change." He picked up a newspaper. A moment later it was whipped out of his hands.

"You're going to get another job," said Mrs. Christmas, firmly.

"Yes, dear, but I thought a few weeks' holiday . . ."

"With reindeer fodder the price it is?" Mrs. Christmas lugged him onto his feet, jammed his hat on his white curls and pushed him smartly towards the door.

"Off you go, young fella-me-lad. No work, no dinner. If you think I'm having you lounging around at home all day, you can think again."

So, Father Christmas wandered miserably down to the Job Shop, where a keen young man was very surprised to be confronted with a rosy-cheeked, white-bearded fat man who described himself on the form as "Freelance Toymaker and Long-Distance Deliveryman."

Still, he did his best.

"If it's a job with good prospects you want, you could try working in a bank," he said uncertainly. "There's a vacancy at the one down the road."

"Jolly good," said Father Christmas.

Next day Father Christmas was sitting in the same seat and looking a bit sheepish as the keen young man listened to the bank manager on the telephone. The bank manager was not very happy.

"A raving lunatic!" he shouted. "He gave away four thousand seven hundred and sixty-five pounds and fifteen pence before we realized what was happening. He even gave away the pens and blowers! Ho! Ho! Ho! indeed! And you should have seen the clothes he wore."

A few minutes later the keen young man put the receiver down.

"Well, that wasn't such a great success, was it? I mean, the Chancellor of the Exchequer isn't going to have to worry about his job, is he?" he said sternly.

"It's in my nature, I suppose," murmured Father Christmas.

The young man was really quite kindhearted, and so he flicked through the job file again.

"Have you had experience of heavy goods vehicles?" he asked.

Father Christmas considered. His sleigh had been quite heavy when all the toys were packed on it—he could hardly push it out of the garage.

"Yes," he decided.

The next day he was looking very embarrassed again, while the young man tried to calm down the manager of the long-distance lorry firm. Fortunately, the man was on the telephone, but you could hear his voice all around the room, he was that angry. At last, the Job Shop man put the telephone down.

"Very good," he said sarcastically. "Tell me, how did you manage to park a sixteen-wheel, thirty-ton lorry on the roof of a three-story house?"

"Isn't that normal?" said Father Christmas. "I always park on the roof."

He looked so hurt that the keen young man relented.

"Look," he said. "It'd help matters a lot if you wore something a bit more . . . er . . . respectable."

"What's wrong with red britches with furry turnups and a pointed hat with a woolly bobble?" demanded Father Christmas. "It's never caused any complaints in the past."

"All right, all right. We'll try once more. There's a Christmas vacancy at the local toy factory. I shouldn't think you could mess that up."

"Well, you messed that up," said the keen young man, who didn't look quite so keen now, as he apologized to the toy factory manager and put down the phone.

"I didn't like making toy soldiers and machine guns," said Father Christmas. "Unpleasant things."

"Yes, but wooden Noah's Arks and teddy bears," said the young man. "What sort of things are they to give to kids? I'm sorry, Mr. Christmas, but you are what we in the trade call 'unemployable,' and I can't think of anything suitable for you."

Father Christmas was just leaving when the telephone rang. The Job Shop man picked it up and listened.

"Oh yes?" he said. "Go on. Fat, you say. Jolly? I see. Ability to say *Ho! Ho! Ho!* an advantage. Well, I'll certainly see what I can do for you. In fact, I think I might have the very man."

"Mr. Christmas," he said, putting down the telephone. "How would you like to work in a department store?"

Father Christmas arrived home whistling and looking very jolly.

"How did the new job go?" said Mrs. Christmas.

"Very well indeed," he said, sitting down at the table. "It's dead easy. I have to sit in this sort of fairy grotto affair, and a queue of children come and tell me what they want for Christmas. I don't quite know why."

"I hope no one complained about your nice red suit it took me so long to make," said Mrs. Christmas.

"No, it's funny, but I got the impression the manager was very pleased with it," said Father Christmas. "He gave me a bonus because of it, and I get a free lunch and two tea breaks. They all know my name, too: 'Hullo, Father Christmas,' they say. Mind you, I can't help wondering what it's all in aid of."

Mrs. Christmas plonked a plate down in front of him and kissed his white curls.

"They obviously just like you," she said.

A Partridge in a
Post Box

On Christmas Day, a large and oddly shaped parcel arrived in the tiny post office of Collip St. Pancras.

Albert Button the postman took one look at it and said: "I can't deliver that—it's much too big! Anyway, what is it?"

"You're not going to believe this," said the Postmaster, "but it's a partridge in a pear tree."

And sure enough, from inside the brown paper and sticky tape came a rustling and grumbling noise such as a small angry bird might make after spending all night in a parcel.

So Albert Button put it on the front of his bike and pedaled all the way up to a big house on a hill, and the door was opened by an extremely beautiful young lady who gave him a tip.

On Boxing Day there was a crate full of cooing noises.

"Express delivery," said the Postmaster. "I understand it's two turtle doves."

The next day, he peered through the basketwork and saw three fat little birds wearing berets and drinking red wine. One of them was playing an accordion.

"I suppose these are the three French hens," said Albert, heaving them onto his bike.

On the fourth day of Christmas . . .

"Her Truelove never thought about the poor old postman," panted Albert, wheezing away up the hill with a parcel containing four very heavy calling birds.

Next day, of course, there were only five golden rings, which the young lady was very pleased with. She smiled at Albert and he whistled all the way home.

He didn't even mind about delivering the six geese which on the following morning were a-laying all over his mailbag. He was more careful with the seven swans a-swimming.

"They can break a man's arm with a blow of their nose," he said.

On the eighth day of Christmas he said to the eight maids a-milking: "Now look, ladies, there isn't no room at all for you all on my bike. I'll just have to carry you one at a time, like, on the crossbar." And he blushed.

By the ninth day Albert had got into the swing of the thing.

"Right then, lads," he said to the drummers, who were standing around rather aimlessly with penny stamps stuck all over them. "All together now—huh-one, huh-two, huh-one-two-three-four . . ."

On the tenth day he rode ahead proudly on his bike while behind him the ten pipers played "Will Ye No Come Back Again?."

On the eleventh day he waltzed, fox-trotted, and tangoed up the hill with the eleven ladies dancing, in particular a rather fetching lady with black hair who gave him a kiss.

But on the twelfth day of Christmas the Postmaster said: "That's right. They've got lost."

"Lost?" said Albert. "Lost? How can you lose twelve lords a-leaping?"

"They're probably a-leaping in a goods siding at Crewe," said the Postmaster. "British Rail has spent all morning looking. They've found all kinds of things, but no lords. They did find a small baron in a letterbox near Bath, but I told them it wasn't one of ours and they put him back."

"This is terrible!" said Albert. "She'll be so disappointed. Perhaps she'll think her Truelove forgot to send them!"

He leapt onto his regulation bicycle and pedaled madly off towards the Head Post Office in Blackbury, where he and all the other postmen—who had all heard about the strange presents—sifted quickly through the parcels.

There was not even one knight, and not so much as the smell of an earl.

Albert Button sat down on a pile of letters with his head in his hands. He looked blearily at the other postmen. There were six. Add the Telephone Manager and his engineers, that's nine, he thought. And the Head Postmaster and his deputy and me makes twelve.

"Gentlemen," he said, standing up, "this is a drastic situation. Is there a place round here where we can hire some silk knee breeches and a dozen coronets?"

On the twelfth day of Christmas the young lady in the house on the hill looked out of her window to see a large trampoline being hauled into position on the front lawn.

"Right, lads!" hissed Albert. "Leap for your lives!"

Up and down they went, spinning in cartwheels and somersaults and figures of eight. *Boing! Spring! Bounce!*

"We're lords," said Albert pointedly, as he sailed past the window upside down. "Make no mistake about it. Ain't we, lads?"

She smiled and waved to them.

On the thirteenth day of Christmas, she got married to her Truelove, and the Best Man—who stood there in his best uniform, his buttons all polished and the five gold rings in his hand—was Albert Button. There was a lord's coronet wedged tightly onto his head. He had to put his cap on over the top of it. But he was smiling.

The New Father Christmas

I n the manager's office of the big Christmas toy factory at the North Pole, complicated industrial negotiations were just about to break down.

"No," said Father Christmas.

"Is that your last word?" said Sean O'Haircut, the head gnome.

"Yes," said Father Christmas, folding his arms.

So Sean O'Haircut blew his shop steward's whistle and went out to the notice board in Father Christmas's huge toy workshop and stuck up the dreaded notice:

Owing to the breakdown of talks between management
(Father Christmas) and the representatives of GELPA
(Gnomes, Elves, Leprechauns, and Pixies Association),
RNRAASP (Red-Nosed Reindeers and Allied Sleigh-Pullers)
and UFJS (the Union of Fat Jolly Snowmen),
a strike is hereby declared.

SIGNED Sean O'Haircut, Works Convenor

P.S.: *Strikebreakers will jolly well get turned into frogs.*
SIGNED Sean O'Haircut

One by one, the machines stopped. The fairy toymakers downed tools, clocked off at the magic cuckoo-clock, and went home.

Father Christmas was sitting with his head in his hands when Jack Frost bustled in with a flurry of snowflakes. "Oh dear," he said.

"We're going to have to cancel Christmas," said Father Christmas. "The reindeers say the sleigh's too heavy with all these extra children in the world, the gnomes say they're over-worked and underpaid—oh dear, oh dear . . ."

"It's that Rudolph I blame," said Jack Frost, frostily. "He is such a red-nose reindeer, after all."

One of Father Christmas's twenty-five telephones rang. It was the BBC. Then someone else rang up. There was a long conversation which mostly consisted of sighs from Father Christmas.

"Someone wants me to go on a television show with Sean O'Haircut and—er, a young lady called Raquel Welch, is it? And a lot of other people. He seemed quite a super fellow for a television man," he said to Jack Frost. "He sounded as if he was a relative of yours."

Soon the horrible news was all over the world: Christmas would be canceled due to industrial disputes. Christmas decorations were taken down, television companies had to think of something to put on the television instead of boring old films, and a lot of little children just cried and cried and cried.

And on top of it all the snow that Jack Frost had specially

ordered for the season fell and made everywhere look as white as the inside of a ping-pong ball—but it was ruined because there were no Christmas robins or fat jolly snowmen—they were on strike.

Father Christmas appeared on the *News at Ten* and said what with profits and the Freeze and everything, he couldn't negotiate, and Sean O'Haircut went on *Panorama* and turned Robin Day into a parrot.

That rather amused Father Christmas who was sitting in front of the fire and watching television.

"I'm getting too old for this lark," he thought. "I'm about four hundred years past retirement age, after all. I think I'll retire to the Costa Bombe and make way for a younger man."

So the next week the new Father Christmas turned up for the job. He was tall and thin and fairly young, with long hair, rimless glasses, and a necklace of Tibetan goat bells. He wore flared red trousers and his beard was quite the oddest thing the goblin toymakers had ever seen.

He sacked the reindeers because his sleigh was peer driven.

He called everybody "man," which really annoyed the elves, and he kept snapping his fingers.

He started to "modernize and streamline" the toyshop, which meant sacking practically everybody and replacing them with machinery because, he said, "modern toys are where it's at, man. No one wants your wooden Noah's Arks."

"This is getting me down," said a snowman called Brown, when the Works committee met in the canteen.

"He keeps wanting me to make working antiballistic missiles, whatever they are," grumbled an old gnome.

"I wonder if we just might have done a silly thing, comrades," said Rudolph, the red-nosed reindeer.

They all looked at Sean O'Haircut, who blushed. "Oh, all right," he mumbled, "I'll go and see the old boy. He wasn't as bad as this one. I'll say that for him."

So it was that early on Christmas Eve Sean O'Haircut arrived on a sun-baked beach on the Costa Bombe, where old Father Christmas was sunbathing in a pair of red swimming trunks.

They had a long chat, and soon they were on a special plane bound for the North Pole.

"Right," said Father Christmas, walking into the toyshop and rubbing his hands, "what's been going on here, then? What's that machine doing? And where are my reindeers? WHO IS RESPONSIBLE FOR THIS?"

Five minutes later there was a terrific row in the manager's office and the new Father Christmas came flying out.*

"Right," said Father Christmas, putting on his red fur-lined jacket and glancing at the clock. "We've only got a few hours; we'd better get a move on."

"Yes, sir!" chorused the elves.

"And what with profits and whatnot I reckon you'll all get a pretty big Christmas bonus," said Father Christmas, who was no fool.

And they did.

---

* Pretty soon he finger-snapped his way into quite a good job managing a pop group called Purple Santas.

The Great Blackbury Pie

This is the story of the great Blackbury pie, and the amazing events that happened in Gritshire on Christmas Day, 1850.

You see, there lived in Blackbury—a pleasant little town really—a millionaire called Albert Wincepartner. He was the mayor, and he had made his money selling rabbits to Australia. He was small, round, and red-faced.

One day early in December he was strolling along the High Street with his friend Blanket, the town clerk.

"You know, Blanket," he said, "at this time of year I can't help thinking about the poor people who won't have any Christmas dinner."

"Ar," said Blanket, who was thinking of something else entirely.

"I reckon," said the mayor, "we should do something. Take a note of this, Blanket. I'll pay for—oh, a hundred pies for the poor of Gritshire, each pie to be a foot across. Pies at Christmas—just right. See to it."

But Blanket wasn't paying attention. When he got back to

his office he told his assistant, who told a secretary who went and told Mr. Gwilliam Plum, a noted baker.

"One pie a hundred feet across?" said Plum. "Are you sure? But—well—a hundred feet across . . . !"

Mr. Plum thought about it. A smile crept across his face. This was his big moment.

Next day he was very busy. He rounded up all the bakers and butchers in Blackbury and told them of his plan.

"It'll be a magnificent pie," he cried. "A King of Pies! The biggest pie there has ever been! A pie so delicious . . ."

A small man in a high black hat and with a thick cigar in his mouth strolled up.

"You don't want cooks," he said. "You want an engineer for a pie that size. My name's Isambard Brunel, and, since I'm not building any ships or railways at present, I think I'll turn my attention to the really hard problem of building a one-hundred-foot pie."

And he did. He cleared a big area on the outskirts of the town and set a thousand men to work to build the biggest oven in the world.

Brunel lit another cigar. "Where," he said, "are we going to get a one-hundred-foot pie dish? It'd have to be the size of a gasometer!"

He looked towards Blackbury Gas Works and grinned. A moment later, fifty men headed in that direction with a large saw.

Meanwhile hundreds of carts were coming up the hill, laden with supplies.

"Five hundred tons of flour," said Mr. Plum, ticking them off on a long list. "Three tons of salt, two tons of pepper, two hundred tons of onions, one bay leaf . . ."

The gasometer was manhandled into place, upside down, and two hundred pastry cooks started to lay the foundations of the pie. Then more carts came, from butchers for miles around, with beef, mutton, chicken, goose, lamb, bacon, and dripping. They shoveled the lot in, and the great lid was lowered into place.

Then Brunel lit the oven with the end of his cigar.

"Amazing!" said Plum the baker, running up to the hastily constructed Pie Office. "I've a telegram here that says the Queen is coming!"

Everyone stood to attention, and Mr. Brunel at once started work on designs for a fifty-foot royal pie slicer.

By now, the pie was a big attraction. While it stood steaming on its great oven, small boys roasted chestnuts in the fire. A fair had grown up around it. Sightseers were taken on tours round the warm crust, for half-a-crown a time, while the Blackbury Voluntary Silver Band played a selection of waltzes.

Mr. Plum went to bed on Christmas Eve, and dreamed of the fame that would be his when Queen Victoria cut the pie. But he woke up sweating.

"Good heavens!" he said, struggling into his trousers. "The eggcup! We forgot about the eggcup."

Down Blackbury High Street ran Plum the baker, in his trousers and bare feet, just as the sun was rising . . .

The great bulk of the giant pie loomed over the town. Plum started to bang desperately on the Pie Office door, and it was opened by Brunel in his nightshirt.

"Wassamatter?"

"We forgot about the eggcup!" panted Plum.

"What's so important about an eggcup?" said Brunel, rubbing his eyes and staring up at the pie. A dull rumble was coming from it.

"You've got to put an eggcup in a pie to let the air out when it's cooking. If you don't, it explodes!"

"Gracious!" By now the sun was up and people were flocking towards the pie ground. Brunel thought about the damage a monster pie could do, and shuddered.

He rushed to the oven and listened. There was certainly something going on inside the thick crust.

"Stand back!" he cried. "I think it's going to—!"

. . . *rumble rumble Rumble RUMBLE*

BANG!

Red-hot pastry scythed through haystacks ten miles away. Molten gravy shot up like a waterspout. A lump of beef and onions took the top off the town hall. Peas whizzed about like bullets. The great top crust—with no eggcup in it—was never seen again, and in Shropshire there was a short sharp shower of suet.

With cries of joy the people of Blackbury grabbed knives and forks and set to, and the town was silent except for the sound of chewing.

Fifty miles away Queen Victoria watched a large, crust-like object sail over Windsor and said: "I don't find that at all amusing."

"Another time," said Brunel, on the church steeple, to Plum who was hanging from the weathercock, just as some seasonal snow started to fall, "I'll just stick to railways."

And he did.

How Good King Wenceslas Went Pop for the DJ's Feast of Stephen

Good King Wenceslas looked out, on the Feast of Stephen.

Behind him the radio said: "Here is the weather forecast. Deep and crisp and even snow is lying round about, especially on high ground. Tonight's frost will be cruel. There will, of course, be a full moon."

Suddenly a movement caught the good king's eye. Far away among the snowdrifts a poor man came in sight, carrying what looked like an empty petrol can. King Wenceslas's old heart was touched.

"Poor wretch," he thought. "He must be in a bad way to be out on a night like this."

He sent for his page, Albert.

"Hither, page and stand by me," said the king. "Yonder peasant, who is he? Where and what his dwelling?"

Albert squinted at the disappearing figure.

"Him? That's Jim Sponge, the disc jockey. Haven't you heard him, sire?"

"Nay. What is a disc jockey?"

"Oh er, well, he's on the wireless and sings and reads out recipes."

"Verily he must be in a bad way if that is all he can do, lad. Anyway, where and what his dwelling?"

"He's got a pad up towards the Forest Fence, sire."

The king thought deeply.

"This is the season of charity and goodwill," he said. "Bring me flesh and bring me wine and bring me pine logs hither. And my muffler."

But Albert soon returned with bad news.

"All we've got in the castle is a packet of frozen sausages, half a bottle of port-type pinky sort of wine, and two Osocosi Smokeless Lumps, sire."

For the trouble was that Good King Wenceslas was very short of money. Every year Parliament only gave him £5 and a half-price railway season ticket. Owing to the latest cut they'd even reduced his birthday salute to 11.5 guns. But he knew his duty. He stiffened his upper lip.

"Pack them up, my boy. We'll go and bring him Yuletide cheer."

Ten minutes later the king and Albert left the damp and drafty castle and plodded towards the Forest Fence. The snow came up to the king's waist and more of it was falling in big white chunks. All that could be seen of Albert was the red bobble on top of his woolly hat.

"Never mind," said the king. "Just think of the warmth and good cheer we are bringing to a humble fellow human being."

"I'm trying to, sire," said Albert, loyally. "But it's difficult, on account of my feet are frozen all the way up to my neck, sire."

"If you walk behind me and put your feet in the holes made by my boots, you'll get along easier. By the way, where are we?"

By now a blizzard was blowing. Albert tried frantically to see through the white curtain. Behind them the snow quickly filled in their tracks.

"We're approximately lost, sire."

They were. They blundered around a bit, and once or twice the king fell into a snowdrift. Then he stumbled into a black and white striped pole.

"Saved!" he cried. "This, if I mistake it not, is a signpost. Climb up it and tell me what it says."

"It says: 'Reduce Speed Now,' sire."

"Um. Well, at least it tells us we are on a road."

"Yes, sire. Sire?"

"Yes, lad?"

"May I get down now, sire?"

They trudged on until their chilblains shrieked for mercy. Then, when the good king fell over for the fourteenth time, the snowdrift instead of making a noise like *serserscrunch!* made a noise like *serserscronk!*

"There's something inside," said the king. And there was. Inside the great big snowdrift was a very large car, a Rolls-Royce as a matter of fact. The king rubbed his frozen hands together.

"I think, Albert, in view of the prevailing conditions, and taking all circumstances into account, weighing the facts and putting two and two together, I must order you to proceed around this vehicle and try the door handles."

Albert did. The car was open. They very soon dug their way in and sat down on the soft leather seats. It was quite warm inside.

"I wonder who this belongs to?" asked Albert. "It's the latest model."

"I'm sure they won't mind. At least we're snug and warm, and have a bit of food, unlike poor Mr. Sponge," said the king.

In fact, at that moment Jim Sponge was just arriving—on foot—at the local radio station, carrying his petrol can.

"What a night to run out of petrol," he told the commissioner.

"Worse than that's happened, Jim, they've lost the king!"

What had happened was that some radio men had gone along to the castle to record the king's Christmas message—and the king wasn't there. Frantic search parties set out at once. People suddenly realized that without the king, ships would go unlaunched, civic buildings unopened, and the only person they could put on their stamps was the Prime Minister.*

"The king's page told the castle cook that they were going out after a poor man. Apparently, they saw some chap walk past the castle carrying a petrol can, and you know what an old softie the king is," went on the commissioner.

"Um," said Jim, looking thoughtful.

Very soon afterwards he was tramping back along the snowy roads with a full petrol can. He dug into the snowdrift that held his Rolls and, as he got deeper, heard voices.

"I spy, with my little eye, something beginning with S."

"Seat? Steering wheel? Snow? Switch?"

"No. No. No. No."

---

* Who was not very impressive.

"Morning, all," said Jim, opening the door. "I thought I'd find you somewhere around here. Move over and I'll drive. Off we jolly well go!"

As the car purred back to the town, Jim explained that disc jockeys were not all that poor, and was astonished to hear that Good King Wenceslas was very poor indeed.

"We shall jolly well have to do something about this," he said.

First of all, he took the pair of them to the poshest restaurant in town, the Sole Bonne Femme, and bought them a slap-up meal, and cigars. Then he took them to the Prime Minister's house.

"If you don't raise the jolly old king's wages, I'll jolly well tell all the housewives about this on the JS Prog," he told the wretched man. "Then they won't vote for you."

"Er . . . well, we never thought about it . . ." said the Prime Minister. "But now that you mention it . . ."

Later on, the king was a special guest on Jim Sponge's show and helped him read out the record requests and recipes.

The stars were coming out as he and Albert walked back to the castle. He was humming snatches of pop songs.

"You know," he said, "Albert, I think this is going to be a good year."

Dragon Quest

This is a revised version of one of Terry's stories which was origi-nally published in the Bucks Free Press *in 1966, and later again in 2014 in the collection* Dragons at Crumbling Castle *(Random House Children's Publishers).*

A very long time ago there was the little hilly kingdom of Grig.* In it lived about a thousand people and five thousand goats, and it was ruled—if that's the word, all things considered—by King Griddlebone the Quite Good.†

One Sunday morning he was sitting up in bed eating an egg when about a dozen page boys trooped in. In those days, of course, there were no newspapers, so the page boys had to remember everything that was going on so they could tell the king.

"Dragons Invade The Crumbling Castle Area," shouted the first page (this was the headline), and then he said in an ordinary voice: "For full details hear Page Three."

* It's probably buried under the sea by now.
† His father was King Griddlebone the Good, but he wasn't so good as his father.

King Griddlebone dropped his spoon in amazement. Dragons! There hadn't been a dragon in the kingdom for years.

After Page Three had told the whole awful story, Page Four added that people were expecting the king to do something about it.

"Throw them out and give them a penny each," said the king to the butler. "Then call out all my knights."

Later that morning he went out into the courtyard and said: "Now then, men, I want a volunteer . . ." Then he adjusted his spectacles. The only other person in the courtyard was a small boy, wearing a suit of chain mail far too big for him.

"Where's everybody else?"

"I don't know, sire. Someone said something about dragons, and everyone decided they felt far too ill to get out of bed. Except me."

"Aha," said the king. "You're not afraid of dragons, eh? Good show. Well, I'll lend you my second-best suit of armor and perhaps you can stop these dragons from rampaging . . ."

So, a little while later, the young knight, whose name was Ralph, whistled cheerfully as he rode a donkey over the drawbridge and disappeared over the hills. When he was out of sight of the castle, he took off his armor and hid it behind a hedge, because it squeaked and was too hot. He put on his ordinary clothes.

All that day Ralph and the donkey followed the winding lane through farmland and neat woods until they reached a forest of oak trees.

"I don't like the look of it," said Ralph doubtfully, eyeing the shadows between the trees.

"Full of wolves and monsters, I shouldn't wonder," agreed the donkey.

"I didn't know you could talk," said Ralph. "Fancy that, by St. Agham! I never heard a donkey talk before!"

The donkey waggled his ears. "By and large, what's a donkey got to talk about?" he said and trotted towards the wood.

They hadn't gone more than a few yards when a great big knight in black armor galloped up to them on a fiery black horse.

"Halt in the name of the Friday Knight, by St. Cernaque!" he bellowed.

"All right, but is this the way to Crumbling Castle?" asked Ralph.

The black knight opened his visor and said in a quite ordinary voice: "Well, yes it is, actually." Then the visor was snapped back, and he bellowed: "But you'll have to fight me first, by St. Magnus!"

The black horse charged forward while Ralph tugged and tugged and tried to get his rusty sword to leave its old leather scabbard. He needn't have bothered because after about three gallops the black knight fell off his horse anyway and landed with a hey-ho rumbelow on his head.

There was silence for a moment and then a small door in the back of the armor opened, and Ralph saw that the Friday Knight was a very small man indeed.

"Sorry," said the knight. "Can I try again?"

"Certainly not," said Ralph. "I've won, because you've fallen down first."

"Quite true. Rule VII/2a, *The Manual of Chivalry*," agreed the donkey.

Ralph looked a bit surprised, but that was nothing compared to the expression on the other knight's face.

"I shall call you Fortnight. 'Cos I've fought you," said Ralph.

There was a great deal of clanking as Fortnight clambered out of his armor and then the two of them went on towards Crumbling Castle. After a while they became quite friendly, because Fortnight was really rather jolly and knew lots of jokes and could sing quite well, too.

Next morning, they came across a wizard sitting on a milestone, reading a heavy book. He wore the normal wizard's uniform: long white beard, pointed hat, a sort of nightdress covered in cabalistic symbols, and long floppy boots, which he had taken off to reveal quite unmagical red socks.

"Excuse me, sir," said Ralph, because wizards are fairly unpredictable. "Is this the way to Crumbling Castle?"

"Oh yes, by St. Transom! But I wonder if you could help me with this little problem?"

He said his name was Pilgarlic and he was sitting by the road because his magical seven league boots had broken down. Magic boots were handy—you could walk miles in them without getting tired—but these needed a bit of attention.

So they gathered round, and since Fortnight knew a bit about mechanics and Pilgarlic knew less than a bit about magic they managed to get one boot working.

"It'll only be a three-and-a-half league boot now," said Fortnight. "You'll have to hop."

Pilgarlic was very grateful and decided to join them on their adventure.

Day by day the land around them grew grimmer and grimmer.

Foggy mountains loomed up on either side of them. Gray clouds covered the sun, and a cold wind sprang up. They plodded on and came to a cave hidden in a clump of thorn bushes.

"We could do with a fire," said Ralph.

"A mere nothing," said Pilgarlic, and produced in quick succession a small hat, a bucket handle, a *trʃgrkxjii* without feathers, a banana, and a brass candlestick. Then he sighed and took a box of matches out of his hat.

After a small meal they dozed off while the fire collapsed into a heap of gray ashes.

Crack! went a stick in the bushes.

Fortnight woke up. Something was creeping towards them. It seemed to have very large feet. An owl hooted, thought better of it halfway through, and changed it into a cough.

"Yield, by St. Caradoc!" said Fortnight, picking up his sword and tripping over Pilgarlic. In an instant there was total confusion. Everyone grabbed a sword and rushed into the bushes, where it was so dark they kept walking into each other and treading on thorns.

"I've got it!" shouted Fortnight and jumped onto something.

"Me!" mumbled Pilgarlic from the leaf mold.

While all this was going on something very small crept out of the bushes and began to warm itself by the fire. Then it sniffed at Pilgarlic's knapsack and ate his tomorrow's breakfast.

"Look, there it is!" shouted Ralph, as they stumbled out of the bushes. "It's a dragon!"

"It's a very weeny one," said Fortnight doubtfully.

It was about the size of a kettle and green and had very large feet. It looked up at them, sniffed a bit, and began to cry.

"Perhaps my breakfast didn't agree with it," muttered Pilgarlic, looking at his rucksack.

"Well, what shall we do with it? It doesn't look very dangerous, even if it is a dragon," said Ralph.

"Has it lost its mommy, then?" cooed Fortnight, getting down on his hands and knees and smiling at it. It hurriedly backed away and breathed some smoke at him. Fortnight wasn't very good with children.

Finally, they made it a bed in the kettle, put the lid on, and went back to sleep.

When they set out next morning, Pilgarlic carried the kettle on his back. After a while the lid opened and the baby dragon stared out.

"This isn't really dragon country," observed Ralph.

"It must have got lost," said Fortnight.

"It's the green variety," said Pilgarlic. "They grow to be seven meters high, and then they go round roaring, rampaging, setting fire to people's houses and generally doing wicked deeds."

"What sort of wicked deeds?" asked Ralph.

"Oh, er, well, I don't really know. Walking on the grass or squeezing toothpaste tubes in the middle, I suppose."

That afternoon they came to Crumbling Castle. It was built on a low hill and surrounded by a little town, and in front of the town was a large moat the local people had made by damming up a stream. But there was no sign of anybody—not even a dragon.

They plucked up the courage to knock at the big black door.

"No one in," said Fortnight as the echoes died away. "Let's go, by St. Tritan!"

"You have a try," said Ralph to Pilgarlic. "Don't you know any opening spells?"

"Certainly," said the wizard. "*Trafgreshipofstaetening! Milograshi! Pootle!* Er, um, I command thee to open in the name of Bretoloxle!"

The door turned a soft pink color. Ralph prodded it, then bit off a bit and tasted it. "Pink meringue," he said.

"My word, dashed tasty door," said Fortnight, after they had eaten their way through.

The courtyard was silent.

"I don't like this much," said Ralph, "I keep getting a feeling something is going to jump out on us."

"That's very nice," said Pilgarlic in a withering tone of voice. His nerves were getting rather frayed.

"It's all right," said Ralph. "Dragons are seldom bigger than the average house or hotter than the average furnace. So come back," he added, treading on the wizard's cloak as he tried to run away.

Just then a large green dragon crawled round the corner and raised its eyebrows when it saw them.

"Good morning," it said, which immediately gave our heroes a bit of a problem, because it's difficult to fight a polite dragon.

"Well, good morning," said Ralph. "Er, excuse me, are you one of the dragons that's been rampaging round and eating people?"

"Only one or two of the more unpleasant ones," said the dragon.

A couple of other dragons wandered up, and one of them said: "I suppose you are the gallant heroes who have come to vanquish us?"

"More or less," said Ralph. "Where are the people?"

"Most of them are hiding in the mountains, the beasts."

"Why, what have they done?" asked Pilgarlic, eyeing the dragon's teeth.

"They kidnapped the Dragon Prince," said the first dragon. "My son. That's why we're teaching them a lesson."

Ralph said thoughtfully: "Was he about a foot high with big feet?"

"A tendency to eat other people's breakfasts?" added Pilgarlic.

And Fortnight reached into the kettle and pulled out the dragon.

"We found him lost, miles away," said Ralph.

And that about ended it. The dragons were so overjoyed at having the baby back they decided to leave right away, although they gave the people of Crumbling Castle several caskets of dragon treasure to make up for the inconvenience.

Of course, there wasn't much they could do about the people they had eaten, but by and large they had been unpopular anyway, so no one minded very much.

"Well, well, an adventure with hardly any fighting," said Ralph, as the three left the castle next day. Everyone cheered as they passed through the gates.

"I'd have shown the dragons a thing or two if there had been," growled Fortnight, and tripped over his sword.

They were still laughing when they disappeared over the hills.

The Gnomes from Home

M r. Humphrey Cosy's trouble started when he built a rockery in his front garden.

It was a splendid affair. He built it out of concrete lumps and planted it with a Kwikgro Garden Centre £2 Choice Rockery Plants Assortment. In front of it was a little pond.

Then Mr. Cosy bought the gnomes. There were three of them. There was a plastic one in a red hat. He sat by the pond. Then there was the concrete gnome, in magnificent yellow trousers. Finally, there was an old stone gnome with a chipped ear and an unpleasant smirk, who was sitting on a bright green frog.

"Right," thought Mr. Cosy, as he went in for his tea, "that'll make old Jones next door go green with envy, him and his thatched bird table."

A week went by.

On Friday, Mr. Cosy came home from the office to find his wife Agnes crouching in the hall and peering through the letterbox.

"Hullo—" he began.

"Shhhh," she hissed. "There's something moving on the rockery!"

"A cat perhaps?" enquired Mr. Cosy.

"No. I think it's a little man in a green hat."

"Mr. Brown at number twenty-six has a sort of greeny-blue trilby—"

"He's three inches high!"

"Oh, I would say on the contrary that Mr. Brown is at least five foot—"

Agnes stood up slowly and advanced on her husband.

"Look," she said, in an odd voice. "Out there on your rockery is a little man in a green hat. He has been there all day. He has walked round all the gnomes. He has got a very shifty look about him. If you don't get rid of him, I shall scream."

And she stormed off into the kitchen and slammed the door.

Mr. Cosy wandered out to the rockery. The little man was sitting on a stone by the edge of the pond, smoking a pipe.

"Evening, squire," it said. "Nice little old day it's turned out to be, eh?"

Mr. Cosy nodded, turned round, and walked slowly indoors. He met his wife in the kitchen. They looked at each other.

"He smokes a pipe," said Mr. Cosy.

"I know," said Mrs. Cosy.

For the rest of the evening, they took it in turns to watch through the letterbox.

"I suppose it's quite rare to have a real gnome turn up on a rockery," said Mr. Cosy, as they went to bed.

"There is that, I suppose. When Mr. Jones next door put up his bird table not even a sparrow went near it for a week," said Mrs. Cosy.

"I mean, it makes our rockery rather select. It rather sets it apart from common rockeries," added Mr. Cosy. "Where are you going, Agnes?" Mrs. Cosy had put on her dressing gown with a purposeful air.

"I'm going to put a saucer of bread and milk out for the little dear," said Mrs. Cosy.

Next morning a sign had been put up in front of the stone gnome. It said:

STATELY GNOMES OF ENGLAND
(P. H. Gimlet, prop.)
See the Amazing Petrified Concrete Grotto!
Marvel at the Terrible Green Frog!
Boat Trips Around the Water Lily!
A Feast of Fun for All the Family!

In addition, a red and white mushroom had grown up by the pond. It had little doors and windows. The little man was sitting outside it in a miniature deckchair.

Mr. Cosy, who had been pruning his roses, read the sign carefully. Then he looked down at the little man, who grinned at him.

"Are you P. H. Gimlet?" asked Mr. Cosy.

"That's me, squire," said the little man. "Of course, this is only a start. What I really want is a wildlife park, that people can drive through without leaving their cars."

Mr. Cosy went and told his wife.

"It'll be nice for him to have some of his little friends along," she said. "I can't see what you are worried about."

There was a knock at the door. On the doorstep was a full-sized man with an embarrassed expression, who said he was from Town and Country Coach Tours. A large luxury coach was parked at the curb.

"We had this telephone call saying we was to run regular coach tours here," said the driver.

He stepped aside so that Mr. Cosy could see the garden and added: "The fare for this little lot comes to twenty-six pounds and the best of luck to you, mate."

The garden was full of gnomes. There were gnomes on the lawn. Gnomes climbed all over the rockery. Baby gnomes were running amok. Several graybeard gnomes were fishing in the little pool. Crowds of gnomes were being taken on conducted tours of the garden ornaments.

"I shan't pay!" screamed Mr. Cosy. "Go and see P. H. Gimlet!"

All that afternoon gnomes kept knocking on the door and asking for drinks of water.

Finally, Mr. Cosy could stand it no longer. He strode out to the toadstool by the pond—or rather he tried to stride but because of the gnome picnic parties and sunbathers that were all round the pond it was more like a hop—and banged on the roof.

"Come on out, P. H. Gimlet, you scoundrel!" he bawled. "I don't like unpleasantness, but I want my garden back!"

The toadstool quivered and the front door fell off.

"These mushroom development places are very badly built. What can you expect, when they put them up overnight?" said

P. H. Gimlet, appearing in his braces. "What can I do for you, squire?"

"Stop turning my garden into an amusement park! I don't like fuss, but if you don't, I'll—I'll tread on your toadstool!"

Mr. Cosy was beside himself with rage by this time, because he had just seen a little notice on his beloved rose bed. It said:

To be erected on this site: 120 Spacious Mushrooms
Contractors: Tinkerbelle Construction Ltd

(P. H. Gimlet, managing director)

"I've a jolly good mind to throw the stone gnomes in the pond," snarled Mr. Cosy.

"Here, you can't do that, they're a regular little gold mine," said Mr. Gimlet.

"How would you like it if a lot of people came tramping all over your garden?"

"Oh, they did," said Gimlet. "They chopped down the wood where I used to live to build a load of houses. Excuse me, I've left the kettle on."

Mr. Cosy sighed and picked his way back through the crowds of gnomes. He noticed a new sign by the pond, which said:

The Magic Yuman Bean Wishing Well

Then he had an idea. He went to his garden shed and for the next half hour there was a lot of hammering. At last, he came out with a large sign and stuck it on the garden gate.

Shortly afterwards there was a very small knock at the door. It was P. H. Gimlet.

"Here, there's lots of people in the garden," he complained.

"Yes, I know," said Mr. Cosy.

"And there's a notice on your gate inviting people to come and see the Pixies' Tea Party."

"I know, I put it there."

"Well, all my customers have gone. They don't like being stared at. And some of them nearly got trodden on!" said the gnome.

P. H. Gimlet stormed off back to the rockery. Mr. Cosy watched him take down his signs and stamp away across the lawn.

Soon the garden was empty. That night Mr. Cosy dug a large hole at the bottom of the garden and buried the three rockery gnomes.

But next day he bought a little concrete mermaid and sat her by the pond.

When he got home in the evening his wife was crouched in the hall again.

"There are about fifteen very small fishy ladies in the gold-fish pond," she hissed.

They both peered through the letterbox.

"Oh dear," said Mr. Cosy.

From the Horse's Mouth

S trange things happen in Blackbury. It may be the climate, or the soil, but things in Blackbury are never quite usual. Like the case of Johnno the horse.

He was owned by Ron Weasel, the last rag-and-bone man in Blackbury. One morning—it was quite a nice one, what with the big red sun climbing up through the mists over the Town Hall and all—Ron went out to the stable to feed Johnno.

It was while he was adjusting the nosebag that a muffled voice said: "A fine morning."

"Yes, very pleasant," said Ron, looking round to see who had come into the stable.

"It was me what said that," said Johnno, in a reproachful voice.

Now Ron was a lot of things that aren't approved in polite circles. He wasn't all that enthusiastic about baths, for one thing, and as for housework—why, it never crossed his mind at all. But he wasn't a fool, and if a horse talked to Ron Weasel he didn't start telling himself he hadn't heard anything.

"Wellwellwellwellwell," he said. "How long have you been able to talk, then?"

Johnno swished his tail.

"You said, 'a fine morning'? I never heard you say that before," Ron went on.

"It's usually been a pretty rotten morning up to now," said Johnno.

Ron thought for a minute. Then he said: "Oh well, are we going on our rounds, then?"

Johnno turned round in his stall and sneered, showing great yellow teeth.

"Aha," he said. "When you thought I couldn't talk it was just on with the old harness and away we go, eh? Not quite so much of the old, 'get into them shafts, you great bag of bones' now, eh? Bit more civil, aren't we? More respect, I sec. Less of the old heyup and whoa. Eh?"

"All right, let's try the Station Road area; we haven't been down there for a long time."

And in fact they got a lot of good stuff, so by lunchtime they pulled into a side street for a nosebag and sandwiches. Ron read the sports pages in the paper.

"Ahem," said Johnno, "I've been thinking. Here's me, been pulling the cart all my life, and never a decent wage, and the old firm couldn't survive without me. Oh, you haven't been a bad boss, I suppose. But I want next week off—or I'll strike. I want to go foxhunting."

"Foxhunting!" gasped Ron. "But that's posh! And I can't ride!"

"Never you mind! Foxhunting it's got to be—or I'll strike!"

So, Ron joined the Blackbury Hunt. It cost him a lot of money, especially since he had to buy a red coat.

"The man in the shop called it hunting pink," he told Johnno when he got home. "Looks as red as letterbox to me."

"Don't worry about a saddle," said the horse, "I'll see you don't fall off. Just so long as they don't have any perishing dogs there. I hate perishing dogs."

"I think there will probably be one or two foxhounds," said Ron slowly.

Next day—and much against his better judgment—Ron dressed up in his hunting outfit and rode off to the Jug and Bottle, where the hunt met. Outside the pub were a lot of other people on horseback, drinking little drinks, and when the man came and asked Ron what he wanted he said, "A brown ale."

"And I'll have a pale ale in a pail," growled Johnno. "And there's too many rotten dogs around!"

"Blimey!" said the man.

The other huntsmen were looking rather oddly at Ron, perhaps because he had left his flat cap on. But at last, the hunt rode off down a lane.

They hadn't gone very far when a horn rang out from a nearby wood. Instantly Johnno bunched his great hooves together and took off like a rocket.

"Yoicks!" he bellowed.

". . . !" thought Ron, because that was all he had time for.

Being a carthorse, and a big one at that, Johnno thundered across the fields, going through hedges where he couldn't jump them, and Ron was bounced around on his broad back like a pea on a drum. The rest of the hunt streamed after them, with the foxhounds yelping.

"Too many rotten dogs spoiling everything!" bellowed Johnno, aiming a few kicks at them.

"You're not supposed to do that!" screamed Ron.

Slowly Johnno drew level with the panting fox.

"Now what?" he asked. "Do we get a prize or something?"

Ron managed to gasp out what was supposed to happen to the fox.

"Never!" swore the horse. "What a rotten idea! Here you, fox, yes, you with the big tail—I'M ON YOUR SIDE!"

The fox glanced up, and then, with a despairing leap, landed on Johnno's back behind Ron.

"Righto!" said Johnno. "Now to show those rotten dogs two clean pairs of hooves!"

And away they crashed over the countryside.

Far behind them the Master of Foxhounds, Lord Cake, was having to be helped down from his horse. His face had already gone red with anger, but the anger had now gone purple with fury and the fury had gone white with rage. But since he doesn't come into the story again . . .

Soon the sounds of the hunt were far behind, and Johnno cantered gracefully though the Gritshire countryside.

"What shall we do now?" he asked.

"I just want to go home," moaned Ron.

"Nonsense! The day's just getting interesting," said Johnno, heartily. "This is much better than dragging that blessed cart around the town!"

He trotted around a wood, and they came to the racecourse.

"Oh no," thought Ron.

"My word!" said Johnno.

It was Blackbury Racecourse, and this was the day of the Gritshire Handicap. Johnno, of course, had come out at the far side of the course, where there weren't many people.

"I can just see myself winning a race," mused Johnno, sticking his head over the railings.

"Oh, no!" thought Ron.

People didn't take much notice of Johnno and Ron—and the fox, who had fallen asleep—as they made their way around the course. After all, the place was full of small men on horseback.

Johnno reached the paddock where the racehorses were and neighed softly. Immediately all the other horses whinnied and rushed up to the fence, where a sort of conversation was carried on in horse whispers.

"I really think we ought to be getting home," said Ron, who was afraid he'd lost control of the situation.

He was wasting his time. When the racehorses were led out of the paddock Johnno trotted resolutely behind them. When the horses lined up at the start, Johnno was in there with them.

"'Ere!" said a jockey.

"What the!" said the starter.

"Hey!" said an official man in a white coat.

Up! went the starting gate.

The racehorses galloped off. Johnno thudded along slowly behind them. Ron turned to look back and saw that a lot of angry-looking men were running along, waving their fists.

Up ahead strange things were happening. Some of the racehorses had slowed down to a walk, or were eating grass, and gazing dreamily at the countryside, while their jockeys looked at each other in bewilderment.

Johnno cantered heavily past them, grinning.

"How did you manage that?" asked Ron.

"Oh, they said it was the least they could do for a poor horse that had to spend his life dragging a big heavy cart round on hard streets," smirked Johnno, as he lumbered past the winning post.

He gritted his big teeth. "Now for the cup!"

He snorted and rushed straight at the table where the Mayor of Blackbury was waiting to present the big silver cup to the winner of the race and, before anyone could move, he seized it in his mouth, turned round, and leapt the fence into the next field.

They hadn't gone far when there was a great commotion behind them. The Blackbury Hunt had reached the racecourse and for a moment Johnno had been forgotten about as dogs barked, officials got bitten, and jockeys and huntsmen milled around in the confusion.

"Home," said Ron, firmly. "And tomorrow I'll return the cup."

"They'll never believe you if you do," said Johnno. "Whoever heard of a talking horse? I won that cup fair and square, well, more or less, anyway."

They reached Ron's rag-and-bone yard when it was dark. Ron shoved Johnno and the fox into the stable, locked the door, and hurried up to bed before anyone saw him.

When he went into the stable next morning, the cup was nestling in Johnno's manger, with the fox asleep by it.

"Not a very nice morning," said Ron.

Johnno said nothing.

"Might clear up later," said Ron, looking thoughtful.

Johnno chewed on a straw.

"I believe you've lost your voice," said Ron. He reached out for the cup and Johnno stamped lightly on his foot.

Ron thought for a bit more. Then he went off and came back with a double ration of mash.

"Take your time over breakfast and then perhaps we'll see about a little bit of work," he said.

He thought: "I wonder, did I dream it all?" Then he looked at the cup again.

Johnno grinned into his nosebag. "Double rations and a bit of respect," he thought. "He's learned his lesson. Life is going to be quite good from now on."

And it was.

Blackbury Weather

I t was an ordinary Saturday afternoon in the little Gritshire
market town of Blackbury.

Ordinary, that is, except that on the Blackbury Rovers
ground, behind the Gridley "Both Ends Meat" Sausage Co. Ltd
factory, the town team was playing East Slate United in the
Cup Final.

After eighty-five minutes it was still a draw. A gasp went up
from the crowd as Jim Sponge, the East Slate winger, took the
ball and whizzed down towards the Blackbury goal.

And at that moment a tiny black cloud formed in the clear
blue sky over the pitch. It hung there for a minute, making tiny
thundering noises, and then shot off after Sponge. It caught up
with him just as he reached the goal and there was a flash
and . . .

BANG!

They found Jim's football boots—with smoke coming out of
them—halfway up the terraces. Jim himself (except for his eyebrows, which took weeks to grow again) was found dazed and

unharmed on the roof of the changing room. They never found the ball.

The mysterious Blackbury weather had struck again!

That night Alderman Maurice Oxford, chairman of Blackbury Borough Finance, General Purposes and Miscellaneous Things Committee, called a special meeting in the Town Hall.

"Last week it rained hailstones, as big as cricket balls, just when the Minister for Interference came down to open the Blackbury Institute of Applied Nonsense," he said. "And I need hardly remind you that on Tuesday we had twelve inches of rain, just when the mayor was opening the new swimming pool. And it only fell on the mayor, too."

He glared around the room. "Something has gone very wrong with the weather in Blackbury, and it's up to us to find out what—"

He stopped and stared, and they all saw what he was looking at. In the center of the room the air was beginning to thicken, and in seconds it formed a little whirling spiral no more than a foot high.

"That is a whirlwind . . ." began Alderman Oxford.

Whoosh! Papers started to fly around the room, and the committee got stuck in the doorway as they all tried to rush out at once.

With great presence of mind Alderman Oxford slammed the heavy oak doors. They all stood in the corridor and listened to the muffled sounds as the little whirlwind buzzed around the room, knocking over chairs and smashing light bulbs.

Up spoke Councillor E. I. Addio, who was also manager of

Blackbury Rovers. "Indoor weather isn't natural," he said. "If you ask me, there is more to this than meets the eye."

"Scatter!" shouted someone.

A little black cloud had formed overhead. Robes flying, the councillors ran down the corridor, turned the corner—and fell into a snowdrift. There was a heavy blizzard blowing between the Clerk of Works Department and the Accounts Office.

Not only that, but to judge by the noise quite an interesting thunderstorm was banging about in the Town Clerk's office.*

Outside, other strange things were happening. Icebergs appeared in the kiddies' paddling pool in the park, while half a mile away, West Blackbury sweltered in a temperature of ninety-six degrees. A gale swept North Blackbury, but in Blackbury New Town the air was perfectly still—and full of giant snowflakes. Strangest of all, a perfect miniature hurricane formed inside a kettle belonging to Mrs. E. Blanket of Mafeking Road, and when she let it out, it roared away over the chimney tops.

Late that night Maurice Oxford, Mr. Addio, and Chief Inspector Charlie Artful, from Gritshire police headquarters, held a special meeting in one of the Town Hall cellars. They all had umbrellas, just in case.

"The Meteorological Office in London has been on to us," hissed Mr. Artful under his breath. "Apparently Blackbury is the only place where this is happening. All this odd weather stops at the borough boundary!"

"Have you got any clues?" asked Mr. Addio, glancing nervously at the ceiling.

---

* In fact, it was chasing him round his desk.

"We've examined the hailstones for fingerprints. But even if someone was causing this freak weather, and we don't know how, I can't see how it's against the law," said the inspector.

"Aha," said Maurice Oxford. "If you found the criminal, couldn't you charge him with causing a breach of the peace? Snowing without a license, perhaps?"

"I dunno," said Inspector Artful, "I just catches 'em, I don't know what happens to 'em afterwards. There is one thing, though. All the places that have had this weather are either in the Town Hall or within line of sight of the Town Hall clock tower. I suppose if someone had some gubbins or other that could alter the weather, he might be aiming it from the tower."

"Gosh," said E. I. Addio. "Have you been up there?"

"Yes, and we found a few cigarette butts. Someone has been up there recently."

Alderman Oxford looked thoughtful. "Whoever it is, he seems to like making the council look foolish," he said slowly. "So I've got an idea . . ."

Three days later there was the Blackbury Mayor–Making Ceremony, when the new mayor for the year took office. It was a very old tradition, going all the way back to 1329. The old mayor and the new mayor had to walk along a plank over the river Um and exchange three bows, and there was a lot of official stuff with scrolls and chains and Cedric the duck.★

Policemen were hidden behind every bush. Chief Inspector

★ The official mascot of Blackbury Corporation; there has been a duck on the official town crest of Blackbury since 1598. No one knows why. Perhaps they just like ducks.

Charlie Artful himself was lurking in the shrubbery around the clock.

Alderman Maurice Oxford was going to be the new mayor, and as the town band struck up the traditional tune "Blackbury Races," he glanced nervously up at the little windows around the clock and thought he saw a shadow. He inched out over the river Um while the crowd cheered.

The retiring mayor, Horace Milparslie, stood staring up at the tower. "Here," he said, "look who's up there! It's—"

Fzzzzzip! A tiny bolt of lightning knocked him into the river, and policemen jumped in all along the bank as the current carried him spluttering away.

The little thundercloud that had attacked the old mayor turned on Maurice Oxford, who slowly backed away. He ducked just in time as it flew over his head and straight into a tuba held by an astonished bandsman, where it made a great din in the pipes.

Maurice Oxford grabbed a trumpet and blew a great blast. "To the clock tower! The mysterious weatherman is up there!" he bellowed.

Of course, a good chase was like meat and drink to the Blackburians. As one man they turned and rushed towards the tower, followed by the band, the town council, Cedric the duck, a wringing wet old mayor and a load of yelling schoolchildren.

The first thing they found was Charlie Artful, frozen solid with his police whistle halfway to his mouth.

"Are you all right?" panted Maurice Oxford.

"Force some whisky between my lips," muttered the chief inspector through the frost. "He got me before I had a chance to recognize him. Brrrr!"

By then someone had spotted a running figure at the other end of the High Street, and they all thundered off again. By the time they reached the end of the High Street, Maurice Oxford was back among the leaders. People were dashing out of side roads to join the chase.

Maurice saw the figure raise some sort of rifle.

Fzzzzip!

A sheet of ice suddenly covered the road, and people started skidding around. But, mayoral robes flying in the breeze, Maurice skated determinedly on.

On they ran, a smaller bunch now but very angry. Down through Slate Road and doubling back along Market Street, through Bodgers Alley—and Maurice Oxford was gaining.

As he ran, he took his mayoral chain from around his neck and swung it round and round. Then he let go. It shot through the air and knocked the strange gadget out of the running man's hand.

"Oh, well done, sir," said someone behind him.

Maurice ran on and picked the thing up. It had a big barrel and lots of knobs and levers on it, and the biggest of them was set to "Ice." Maurice switched it to "Whirlwind," pointed it at the running figure, and pressed an interesting-looking blue lever.

Fzzzip!

Kicking and struggling the running man was lifted up and over the streets of Blackbury. The breeze blew him right over the Um, and when he was about over the muddiest bit, Maurice switched the machine off.

Splash!

The man came up gasping and everyone shouted: "E. I. Addio!"

"I thought it might be him all along," said Maurice later. "After all, he is manager of the Rovers. And he's never been made mayor, which is why he doesn't like the council. I think he must have left the machine switched on in the clock tower when he was with us."

"Very clever of him to have invented it," said Charlie Artful. "Er, where is it, by the way?"

Maurice said rather too innocently that he didn't know.

But later that evening someone tied a rifle-shaped machine to the weathercock on the clock tower and set it to "Sunny."

Maurice had the best weather ever for his year in office, until the batteries ran out.

The Blackbury Jungle

This is the story of the Blackbury Jungle. It happened, like most things in Blackbury happen, at ten past three in the afternoon.*

Anyway, on this sunny afternoon, Blackbury Borough Council met in the high-ceilinged, dusty, oak-lined town hall. One item on the agenda was the park.

"Now it seems to me," said the mayor, Alderman Amos Stepforward, "we need a bit more color in Blackbury. More flower beds and the like. Brighten the town up and attract more tourists. We could have a Battle of Flowers like they do in the Channel Islands."

"I didn't think flowers were all that warlike," said the councillor Eli Prune, who was half asleep.

"Yes, well, hurrrmph," said the mayor, frowning at him.

* Everything in Blackbury happens at that time because the town hall clock stopped at ten past three one day in 1869.

"Anyway, I propose we send out the park keeper to buy a few seed packets and make a start."

So, the next day the park keeper, Bert Juggins, sent off for a collection of seeds suitable for planting out in Blackbury's rather poky little park, which was all green railings and rhododendron bushes.

What he received was a strange green parcel containing only about thirty seeds. There wasn't even a stamp on it, or the name of the quite reputable seed merchants he had sent off to.

"Well, I'll give them a try," Bert said. "I must say they look rather big for flower seeds."

He scratched thirty holes in the flower beds, dropped in the seeds, watered them from the municipal watering can and went home.

After dinner he went to get his pipe out of his jacket and realized that he had left it in the tool shed in the park. His cottage was on the edge of the park, behind some trees, so he got a torch and hurried across the moonlit lawns towards the shed.

But there was something very different about the park . . .

It was half past midnight, and Mayor Stepforward was fast asleep. Suddenly there was a clatter at the window, just as if someone had chucked a handful of gravel at it.

The mayor stumbled out of bed, pushed open the window and mumbled, "Wassat?"

"It's me, Mr. Mayor," said the park keeper, jumping up and down excitedly. "You've got to come down! The park's gone mad!"

"Mad?" said the mayor.

"Everything's growing!"

"So I should think!" said the mayor. He shut the window and got back into bed. "What else do you expect in a park?" he muttered before falling asleep.

Down below Bert wrung his hands nervously and ran off to find someone else.

Meanwhile the park had completely disappeared under a rapidly growing pile of green stuff. Great snaky tendrils whipped up and caught the railings, while enormous tree trunks whizzed up like rockets, exploded into leaf, blossomed, and then produced great big purple fruits. A vine was already creeping up the roof towards the town hall clock.

The mayor woke up in the morning because something was tickling his nose. It was a big yellow flower on the end of a tree branch that had grown through the window. Several other bushes had broken into the room.

"Goodness!" he cried, sitting up, and a large green melon plopped onto his head.

He had quite a fight to get his trousers away from a green thorn bush, and as for his hat, it was up near the ceiling on the end of a creeper. He couldn't get out of the front door—it was quite overgrown—so he had to climb out of the window.

Blackbury could hardly be seen under all the plants, which were still growing. Flowers, fruit and vines were everywhere. The mayor met the postman sitting on a branch eating a banana. He asked him what had happened.

"It all just grew," said the postman. "Have a banana?"

Blackbury was hidden under a mound of green. Creepers and vines flourished everywhere. Great big trees grew in the High Street—and as for flowers, there were gigantic red, white and purple orchids growing out of every gutter, and sprays of yellow blossoms on the roof of the town hall.

The mayor made his way across the town as best he could. Often he couldn't get any further on the ground and had to heave himself, puffing and grunting, up trees and walk along branches.

A lot of Blackburians had come out and were poking wonderingly at the undergrowth. One or two of the more enterprising ones were cutting themselves bunches of bananas and grapes.

"I think I could grow to enjoy this," said the mayor, grabbing the end of a creeper and trying to measure the distance to the next branch. "I wonder if I could swing across, like Tarzan of the Apes? You're as young as you feel—"

A moment later he was sitting on a pile of ferns, clutching his head. Bert Juggins was sitting next to him, groaning. "Sorry, I didn't see you coming the other way," he said.

"Oww! My head! Now I know what a conker feels like!" muttered the mayor. "Well, Bert, this is a fine mess you've got us into with those seeds!"

"I don't reckon the seeds I got were the right ones," said Bert. "I mean, I ordered hollyhocks and daisies and things like that—not banana trees."

"We can't have Blackbury looking like an overgrown greenhouse," said the mayor. "What are you going to do about it?"

"Do?" said Bert, plucking a big blue plum from a nearby bush and biting it. "Do you know how much fresh fruit costs these days? We could make a fortune. And we could organize safaris through the High Street."

"Hmm," said the mayor, thoughtfully.

That afternoon Blackbury Borough Council met in the town hall. It was a bit difficult, though. Even finding the town hall among all the jungle that had mysteriously grown up was difficult. Councillor Eli Prune got lost in a thicket of bamboo, for example, and the mayor himself had a very sticky time with a gum tree.

The councillors all sat around on branches or tufts of moss. Several of them were eating plums and melons cut from the vines that festooned the room.

The mayor explained Bert's idea of selling all the fresh fruit and organizing safaris through the jungle to attract tourists. Everyone thought it was a good idea.

No one was really bothered now about how the jungle had arrived. Blackburians soon get used to anything. Within a day or two, it was quite usual to see old ladies going shopping by swinging from tree to tree on creepers, and Blackbury High School moved to the branches of a large elephant tree.

Lorry after lorry loaded with fresh pawpaws, grapes, jungle plums, green melons, and coconuts left one end of the town, while coachloads of tourists arrived at the other.

One trouble was that there were no actual wild animals in the jungle, except perhaps the town hall cat, which was always pretty angry. But the mayor solved that by giving impressions of animal noises from behind bushes, while Bert the park keeper dressed up in a rather musty gorilla outfit. It wasn't a very good one. One tourist, a zookeeper, said sarcastically that it was the only gorilla he had seen with a zip all down his back. But most people were quite happy.

After a week of this the town council met again. Blackbury was making thousands of pounds a day!

"This is marvelous," said the mayor, rubbing his hands together. "And tomorrow we've got a special large party of tourists arriving!"

But something else was going to happen tomorrow, too.

Like many people, the mayor had moved out of his house, which was buried under a mound of greenery, and had built a treehouse in the branches of a huggermugger tree. While he was watching the tourists, Bert the park keeper climbed up a vine with a battered green envelope in his mouth.

"I found this hanging in a banana tree in the park," he mumbled. "It's the packet those seeds came in. It's not a proper seed packet at all!"

The mayor looked at it. In yellow and purple writing, it said:

IMMEDIATE JUNGLE SEEDS
Plant in warm place.
Danger: plants grown from these seeds
seldom last longer than seven days.

"Well, what about it?" said the mayor, leaning against a branch. It snapped, and it was only because Bert caught him that the mayor didn't fall out of the tree.

"I've been looking around," said Bert. "Half the trees are as dry and light as bits of paper already. We'd better warn people!"

"Do you think they'll ask for their money back?" said the mayor anxiously, as they climbed down the tree. A very large branch dropped on his head—but instead of hurting him it just puffed into a cloud of dust. By the time they reached the ground, dust and bits of dry twig were raining around them.

The whole jungle was curling and creaking and popping into dust. The houses of Blackbury appeared again as if by magic. All the tourists thought it was marvelous, of course, and were taking photographs like mad. The mayor shook his head sadly.

"Bang go all the tasty fruits," he said. "Everything's just turning into powder. It'll cost us a packet to clear all this up!"

"The vines and the flowers were enjoyable, yes," said Bert. "But frankly, I think I prefer Blackbury the old way."

"Me too," said the mayor.

"Come on, let's go home."

The Haunted Steamroller

Once upon a time there was a haunted steamroller. It happened like this.

One of the machines in the Blackbury roadworks department was a large maroon steamroller, one of the old-fashioned kinds with lots of brass knobs and copper pipes. It was called J22, which was its works number.

But, of course, it was old-fashioned and used up quite a lot of coal, and it was a bit of a job keeping it bright and shiny.

One day the Mayor of Blackbury said, "That old steamroller is past it. I really think it's time we scrapped it and got one of these diesel ones."

The borough surveyor agreed. But then he said, "Old Bert isn't going to like it. He's driven J22—oh, for years and years, ever since I was a little boy."

And that was quite true, of course. Old Bert Nettle had driven the steamroller for ages, and he was the only council workman who bothered to keep J22 brightly polished. He was very old-fashioned himself, with droopy gray whiskers, a big silver watch on a chain, and a moleskin waistcoat.

The mayor had a think. "Old Bert must be about seventy," he said. "Time he retired, for his own good. It can't be very healthy, what with all that smoke and oil. And we could give him a nice gold watch."

Old Bert heard about this later in the day, when he drove J22 in from a spell of road rolling. He was horrified. What they didn't realize was that Bert's one interest in life was working on the old steamroller.

Bert went home and went to bed early, after damping down the fire in J22. Half the shelves in his little kitchen were full of polish tins and special steamroller grease.

J22 stood in the dark council garage with the dustcarts. The church clocks all round Blackbury struck midnight.

There was a sizzle, and a clank from the firebox. Very, very slowly, the old steamroller's flywheel began to turn. Then it gave a triumphant *chuff* and chugged forwards.

Crash! went the garage door as J22 smashed through it and ran through the empty streets. People threw open their bedroom windows in amazement as the steamroller trundled past with sparks coming out of its chimney.

Old Bert woke up as the steamroller clattered down the High Street.

"This is a rum do!" he thought, tugging on his trousers. "Someone's stolen my steamroller." Two minutes later he had leapt on his bicycle and was pedaling furiously after J22, which was heading for open country.

After a while it was easy to see where the steamroller had

been by looking out for flat hedges, lamp posts, and . . . well, in one place there was a telephone box that was about fifty yards long and one-eighth of an inch thick!

By breakfast time, Bert was high up on Even Moor, north of Blackbury. It was already very hot, and he couldn't find the steamroller tracks any more. He'd just sat down for a rest when a police car pulled up beside him. The mayor was sitting in the back.

"What on earth's happening?" he asked. "The police are everywhere! Have you seen the steamroller?"

"No," said Bert. "But I think it was heading in this direction."

"Dangerous thing, stealing steamrollers," said Chief Inspector Jones, who was driving the car. "Hop in, Bert."

"It's daft, I know," said the mayor, as they drove away. "But some people who saw it go past said there wasn't anyone driving J22!"

"What puzzles me is there was hardly any coal or water on board," said Bert. "She should have run out of water hours ago."

Now remember, this is Gritshire. If it was anywhere else people would start making all kinds of odd explanations, but in Gritshire—and particularly around Blackbury—strange things happen every day and people are more sensible.

"Magic . . ." said the mayor. "Oh dear!"

"She must have heard the surveyor say she was going to be scrapped, so she ran away," said Bert. "Poor old girl."

"That's all very well, but supposing she runs someone over," said Chief Inspector Jones. They all thought about the telephone box.

Most of Even Moor was bare and windswept, with little

woods of gnarled trees here and there. There was nowhere for even a small steamroller to hide.

Then they saw it. J22 was on the edge of one of the woods, plucking branches off the trees with what looked like a trunk and stuffing them into her firebox, for all the world like an elephant eating. As soon as she saw them, she gave a hoot and puffed away between the trees.

"Good heavens!" said the mayor.

"That thing like a trunk was the extension water hose," said Bert. "Come on."

"Well now," said Chief Inspector Jones, "call me a coward if you like, but I'm not sure I fancy coming face to face with a mad steamroller. I think we had better get reinforcements."

An hour later there came a report from the little village of Stoke Cangle, just north of the moor. A steamroller had pushed down the wall of the coal merchant's yard and had stolen a ton of best anthracite. The coal merchant was very angry because the roller had carefully picked him up on the end of its hose and sat him on the roof of his house.

Further north the pursuit party caught up with J22, sucking up water from a pond by the road.

The chief inspector had called up a large breakdown wagon with a big crane on it, and there were several lorries loaded with equipment. Bert was a bit upset by it all.

"What are we going to do?" he asked.

"Well, PC Peddle is going to try and hook a chain round the roller's back axle so we can tow it to Blackbury," said the chief inspector.

"And then poor old J22 will be broken up for scrap," said

Bert, shaking his head. "It doesn't bear thinking about. We used to roll out Blackbury's roads together when the town was hardly more'n a village. I recall one Christmas, 1924 I reckon it was, when we took the Bishop of Blackbury and all the choristers round carol singing because the snow was so deep." He blew his nose, overcome with emotion.

The mayor patted him on the back. "Never mind," he said kindly, "you've got to remember, Bert, this is 1973. Steamrollers are not fashionable any more. But we shall get a nice new diesel one and, I'll tell you what, you can have the first drive on it."

Bert looked slyly at the mayor. "It'll be a dangerous job, putting a hook round her ankle—I mean axle. You'd better let me do it. J22 knows me, after all."

The chief inspector looked a bit doubtful, but he let Bert walk towards the roller, which was still slurping water out of the pond. J22 began to puff uneasily as he approached, but he patted one big wheel and said, "Easy now, girl."

Then before anyone knew what was happening, he leapt aboard the roller and pulled a big lever. Steam hissed in all directions, smoke filled the air and J22 rumbled off up the road. All the astonished people could hear in the din was Bert laughing and shouting: "Go back to be retired? Not us!"

Of course, steamrollers don't move all that fast, but they are very difficult to stop. No one felt inclined to try, anyway. So, the two of them chugged down off Even Moor and headed north.

Bert found he didn't have to steer. J22 was steering herself perfectly, and even stopped when Bert wanted to get down—to buy a pound of sausages in one place, and a packet of tobacco in another—as neatly as you like.

The big flywheel spun round, the great road wheels trundled, and Bert sang as he fried sausages on J22's firebox. He didn't know where they were going, but he felt very happy.

But the mayor and the chief inspector, back in Blackbury, were very worried.

"Officially, of course, Bert has stolen the steamroller," said the mayor. "Of course, we wouldn't do anything about that. But I think they should be stopped, for his own good."

"They're still heading north," said the chief inspector, looking at the map. "I wonder where they're going? By this afternoon they should be driving through the town of Dewley. Perhaps we could stop them there, but how do you stop a steamroller?"

"With another one," said the mayor. "They've got one of those new diesel rollers in Dewley. If they parked that across the road, that'd stop them and no mistake!"

So, when J22 chugged through Dewley, Bert saw the other roller. It was big and green, and looked very heavy. The mayor and a lot of worried-looking people were standing behind it.

Bert shook his head and pulled the brake lever. But J22 chugged on, and only sizzled to a halt a meter away from the roller.

"Look, Bert, you've made your point," cried the mayor. "Why don't you come down now, there's a good chap."

But J22 was moving again . . . *Boing!* The two rollers met with a crash that shook J22 all the way to her pressure gauge. The man on the green steamroller laughed nastily. It was obvious the big roller wasn't going to move—in fact, it was pushing J22 backwards.

Then J22 hooted with three long blasts. The green roller stopped and whistled, which puzzled its driver, because he hadn't touched anything. Everyone gasped as the green roller started to back away very politely.

J22 hooted again, revved up a bit to make sure everything was all right, and trundled on. The mayor had to leap out of the way.

Soon J22 was thundering along with a crowd of angry people chasing her. Bert was quite bewildered by the whole thing. It seemed as though J22 had asked the other steamroller to get out of the way.

Since J22 wasn't too fast, even at top speed, the crowd behind was catching up. She was heading towards a pair of big iron gates, set in a wall just the other side of the town. It was a good job they were open, because she whizzed straight through and on up a wide gravel drive that led to a great big country house.

There were stone sheds built round it and standing outside them were—steamrollers.

There were dozens of them: big red ones, traction engines in all colors, showman's engines with glittering canopies and polished brass thingamajigs—all with steam up. The air was full of the smell of hot oil.

A tall thin man in a very expensive suit came hurrying across the yard to J22, who had stopped. He put his glasses on and, ignoring Bert, peered at her excitedly.

"I say," he said. "I do believe this is a double cylinder brass-boilered J-model roller from the old Snobbut and Munchapple factory!"

"Why, yes," said Bert, surprised to find someone who knew so much about steamrollers. The tall man shook him warmly by the hand.

"I'm Lord Hugh, of Dewley," he said. "And this is my new Steam Engine Museum. We're opening to the public tomorrow. I could just do with this machine to complete my collection. I must say it's in splendid condition. How much do you want for it?"

"Well I—" began Bert, but just then the mayor and everyone caught up, and began talking at once.

Lord Hugh took them all indoors and, after a large tea of strawberries and cream, the mayor found himself holding a check for quite a lot of money—certainly enough to buy a diesel roller for Blackbury—and J22 was being driven off to Lord Hugh's workshops to be given a good clean-up.

"The trouble is," said Lord Hugh, "there just aren't enough people around now who really understand steamrollers. I've been looking for a chief mechanic for months."

"Well now," began Bert, modestly, and very soon—you've guessed it—he was fitted out with a uniform and got the job. Everyone else went away happily, if a little puzzled. But Bert went to look at J22 before he went to bed.

The old steamroller was in a big shed with a lot of others and looked quite at home. So, he just said, "Goodnight," and shut the door.

The Money Tree

Mr. Rupert Wrist's wife wanted a television set.

That was a bit of a problem for Mr. Wrist. He was an assistant joke writer in a matchbox label factory and, believe me, jobs like that are interesting but not very highly paid.

"I'm fed up with having to go and watch Mrs. Jones's down the road every time there's something good on," said his wife.

Then one day, Mr. Wrist saw a little advert in the paper. It said:

Make Money In Your Spare Time!
Yes, You Can Make £££s for just a Few Hours' Work a Week
Send a £1 postal order for details.

Feeling a bit of a Charlie, Mr. Wrist sent off a £1 postal order and then forgot about it. But about a week later a very small parcel arrived. Inside was one seed, and a label saying "Plant In A Damp Place."

"You've wasted your money," said Mrs. Wrist when he told her.

Rupert Wrist shook his head. "The paper said you could make £££s for just a few hours' work, so it must be true. Anyway, I've planted it by the compost heap."

"Just so long as it doesn't turn out to be one of them giant man-eating runner beans like in that horror film we saw," said Mrs Wrist. And that was that.

For days afterwards Mr. Wrist used to go to look at the patch of ground as soon as he got home from work. But nothing grew, except weeds, and pretty soon he got fed up with it.

One warm evening he was taking a stroll among his cabbage plants and watching the sunset when he heard a faint rustling noise.

The seed had sprouted. A spindly green stem was swaying above the weeds. As Mr. Wrist watched, it unfolded another thin leaf and grew at least another inch.

"Here, Rita, come and look at this," he shouted to his wife.

By the time Mrs. Wrist arrived the plant was three feet high and throwing out leaves in all directions. It filled the garden with a strange crackling noise, rather like someone wading through tissue paper.

"I don't like it," said Mrs. Wrist, shivering. "It's definitely got a nasty look about it to me. Next thing we know it'll be crawling across London and tearing down Big Ben, like the thing in the film."

"What I want to know is, how can you make money with it?" wondered Rupert Wrist, lighting his pipe. "I know a bloke at work whose brother makes a bit of money growing mushrooms in his cellar. Or cut flowers. We could sell cut flowers. But this looks more like a bush."

The stem was now ten feet high and had stopped growing upwards. Instead, it was sprouting a crown of branches. They grew and spread across the night sky until the Wrists were standing under a large tree.

"Apples, perhaps. Or pears. Or even peaches," thought Mr. Wrist.

"If we wake up dead in our beds don't blame me," said Rita.

But neither of them got much sleep that night. They lay in bed staring into the darkness and listening to the little crackling and popping noises in the garden. Finally, Rupert could stand it no longer. He leapt out of bed and opened the window.

The tree was in flower. Giant, intricate blooms gleamed in the moonlight. They were beautiful.

"It's cut flowers, then," he thought. "Well, they certainly look nice. Perhaps I can sell them to a florist."

The flowers had a scent. He went back to sleep with it filling the room. "Funny," he thought before he dropped off, "it doesn't smell like you'd expect. Smells a bit like . . . um . . . like banks."

In the morning the tree jingled in the breeze. Its boughs were bent under the weight of its fruit. Most of the flowers were gone. Mr. Wrist went out in his dressing gown to look at it.

Something hit him on the head. There was another gust of wind, and fruit rained down on all sides. Except that it wasn't exactly fruit.

"It's money! Well, I'll go to the foot of our stairs!" gasped Rupert, sitting down.

Coins kept falling off the branches. Most of them were 1p

and 2p pieces, but there were several 50p coins that were almost ripe.

He staggered into the kitchen and tugged his wife through the door. "You won't believe me if I tell you, so come and look," he said.

They stood looking up in wonder, ankle deep in money. True, some of the coins were a bit speckled and most of them were copper. But it was still a good crop.

Mr. Wrist didn't go to work that day. Instead, he counted money. There was £20.13 already ripe. Next morning another £25 was tinkling on the branches.

"It's a pity there isn't more silver," said Rita. "It's no fun having to cart all this to the bank."

"Hmm, I was thinking about marrows," said Mr. Wrist, lighting a cigar.

"Marrows? What about them?"

"Well, if you want bigger marrows, you feed the plant. With fertilizer and . . . er . . . manure and so forth. Shall we try?"

So he bought a bottle of Gianto Wonder Plant Food and poured it around the tree.

Next morning there was quite a heavy crop of 5p coins. And there was one large bud which slowly opened to reveal, still crinkled and slightly damp, a £1 note.

"We're on the right track," said Mr. Wrist. "Still, when you get down to it, 5p pieces are a bit tiring to pick up."

So that evening he put two bottles of Gianto and a barrow-load of horse manure around the tree.

Next day's crop was mainly 50p coins, though perhaps some

of them were a bit weedy-looking. There were several slightly smudged £1 notes.

"I should leave well alone. Overfeeding it might be bad," warned Rita.

"I'm not asking for much. All I want is one crop of fivers, just one. I don't care if it goes back to 1ps after that," said Rupert.

He used an old tin bath as a mixing bowl and prepared a special mixture of twenty-seven different plant foods.

"Right," he thought, as he went to bed, "that should do it."

All night long the money tree shook and shivered.

In the morning there was but a withered stump and one blackened branch bearing a rather inferior and dull penny.

The Wrists watched it gloomily. It fell off.

"Bang goes all hope of being a millionaire. I wonder if my old job's still going?"

He wrote to the advertisers, and they wrote back a rather sarcastic letter saying that what they had sent him was a mushroom-growing outfit, nothing more, and if they knew how to grow money they wouldn't waste their time selling mushroom kits, would they?

There was just enough money left for a television set, so they bought one. And Mr. Wrist planted the last penny.

About a week later he was moodily tying up his dahlias when he saw the penny sprout. Up came a little plant, no higher than his knee. It produced a couple of sweetly scented daisy flowers which blossomed for a few hours, and then it shriveled up.

Mr. Wrist sighed and went and mowed the lawn. It seemed just about the best thing he could do.

The Blackbury Thing

Very late one night, Police Constable Ronald Biddle, Gritshire Constabulary, was proceeding along the quiet, foggy streets of Blackbury when he heard a funny whistling noise.

"'Ullo, 'ullo, 'ullo, what's all this 'ere," he thought, staring up into the frosty sky. Up among the stars shone a red dot. And it was growing bigger.

"Fireworks," he thought. "Funny, it's only January."

The whistling noise rose to a jet scream.

"On the other 'and it may be an aircraft," thought PC Biddle.

Now flames could be seen around the dot, which was hurtling towards Grumble's Wood just outside the town.

"Or a rocket or a balloon," PC Biddle thought.

CRUMP!

Dogs barked. Dust fell down from mantelpieces all over Blackbury. Several bats fell out of a belfry and the Town Hall clock struck seventeen.

There was a great glow over Grumble's Wood. Within

minutes the constable was pedaling furiously along the darkened lanes towards the wood, in a perfect hail of leaves and splinters.

When he got there most of the wood was just a great big hole, full of smoke and steam. At the bottom of it—

PC Biddle squinted through the haze. There was a large glowing object in the bottom of the crater. He stared at it.

Behind him he heard the felonious sound of an official police bicycle being stealthily stolen. "Oi!" he bellowed, turning round.

But by now the mysterious thief was well on his way into Blackbury.

Next morning there was a very different scene round Grumble's Wood. For one thing it was snowing. There were several police cars and a Land Rover from Blackbury University. There was a lot of commotion around the hole.

"Whatever it was, it was spotted by astronomers all over the world," Dr. Jasper Blot was saying.

"Funny to think it came all that way just to drop on old Grumble's Wood," said Chief Inspector William Jones. "Er, just what job have you got at the University, Doctor?"

"I lecture in knitting and domestic economics, actually. All the science staff are away, so they sent me. Blowed if I really know why."

The thing was, the object in the hole was still red hot. There were some rather odd markings on it.

"Did you see *The Ghastly Thing From Dr. Death's Horror Plane* that was on at the Odeon last week?" asked Jones. "This thing came out of a spaceship, see, and it ate—Oh well, anyway, the film started just like this. I think I shall lock my greenhouse tonight. Do you think something came out of that and stole PC Biddle's bicycle?"

Before Dr. Blot could answer, there was a buzz from the radio in Jones's police car. He switched it on.

"We've found something very odd out on the East Slate Road," said the radio. "Something's broken into a greengrocer. We think you better come and look, sir."

Something had smashed the window of the shop and had stolen twenty-three cabbages. But that wasn't the strangest thing. In the snow outside the shop there was just one very large, long footprint. There was another several yards away. And another further on still.

"Oh dear," said Chief Inspector Jones. "Oh dear, oh dear, oh dear."

All that day police tramped after the giant footprints, until they lost them in the bushes on Blackbury Common.

Next day the morning papers were full of headlines like: BLACKBURY OUTER SPACE HORROR SHOCK!

And on Friday even the *Blackbury Gazette, Journal and Weekly Post** had a headline between the auction notices on the front page which said: "Curious Mystery of Giant Footprints Puzzles Police," which was about as excited as the paper ever allowed itself to be about anything.

The police station started getting telephone calls from people who said they'd seen strange green men wandering around. Or purple men. Or big blue spiders.

* Estab. 1867. Premier Advertising Medium for North Gritshire. Rates on applctn.

"It wasn't a big blue spider that stole PC Biddle's bicycle; its feet would never be able to turn the pedals," thought Mr. Jones.

Then a patrol car was called round to the home of Mrs. Edna Bucket, who said she'd been frightened by a "great hairy monster."

"It came leaping over the fence just as I was putting out the washing," she said.

The chief inspector called in Dr. Blot. "This is the first full description we've got of the Thing," he said. "It's large and hairy, with long ears and one leg. And a tail."

"And it must eat cabbages," said Dr. Blot.

"And according to Mrs. Bucket it can jump over a clothesline. Perhaps it comes from some low-gravity planet with a lot of cabbages on it."

That night something large and hairy bounded along a dark street and knocked a policeman's helmet over his eyes.

Next day the army was called in, and a lot of experts from the Ministry of Defence started poking at the mysterious thing in Grumble's Wood. A lot of reporters came up from London.

And that afternoon PC Biddle discovered his bicycle. It was leaning against a fence on his beat, and someone was pumping up the tire.

"What's all this then?" he said in his regulation voice. "Soapy Fred, I do believe."

Soapy Fred was a well-known Blackbury poacher. He straightened up and—seeing a glint in PC Biddle's eye—nodded his head.

"All right, Ron, I snitched it," he said. "I just wanted to get out of that wood quick."

"Grumble's Wood? What were you doing there?"

"Watching pheasants, in a manner of speaking. And then that thing landed not a hundred yards away."

"In that case," said PC Biddle slowly, scratching his chin, "what's this Thing that's terrorizing the town?"

Already the soldiers that were patrolling Blackbury had found some more giant footprints in the snow. They led again to the thick bushes on Blackbury Common, which were soon surrounded by tanks and guns.

At about the same time a very worried lady was in the little village police station in East Slate, ten miles away.

"I run the Retirement Home for Sick Performing Animals in Grubbs Lane, and I want to report a stray animal. I can't find him anywhere," she said.

"And what would be the nature of this said animal?" said the policeman, licking his pencil.

"It was the big bang over towards Blackbury the other night that must have frightened him. He jumped right over the wall," she went on. "He's a kangaroo. His name is Babo. But the poor thing has only got one leg. He had an accident when he was just a little—"

The constable was having a quick think. "Excuse me, madam. I think I'd better make a telephone call," he said.

About an hour later the lady came out of the bushes on Blackbury Common leading a rather small and sorrowful kangaroo. Very quietly, without catching each other's eyes, everyone else went home.

And up in Grumble's Wood, late that night, a large tentacled Thing with purple skin and three eyes climbed down from the tree where it had spent the last few days. And sidled over towards the globe in the crater. It pressed a few lumps on the outside, and when a hidden door opened it climbed in.

"I shan't come here for my holidays again," it thought. "These human beings are crazy."

A few minutes later there was the sound of a motor starting up, and, just as the sun came up, the little round spaceship rose out of Grumble's Wood and very soon disappeared into the clouds.

Mr. Brown's Holiday Accident

It was a fine summer morning, and Mr. John Brown was off on his holidays. Well, half-off really, because he was stuck in a traffic jam halfway to the coast.

"Fourteen whole days without having to work for Trouser, Trouser, Middling, and Fedge," he thought. "Blowed if I'm going to spend them stuck in a queue!"

Then he did something which, in view of what happened later, was really terrible and upsetting. He drove off the main road and down a little tree-lined lane. He was quite surprised at himself, because he'd normally never dream of such a thing. Still, the birds were singing and the blossom was out, and the car bowled along happily.

Until he hit something, in the middle of an empty road. There was a horrible tearing noise.

When he opened his eyes, the orchards, hills, and sky were gone. Ahead of the car stretched a concrete plain, littered with piles of wood, lights, and lorries. Small men were running towards him.

It was as if the car had gone straight through a tall thin wall.

"It must be a builder's yard—perhaps I'd better just carefully go away," he thought, putting the car into reverse. He looked over his shoulder, and then saw the wall. The sky, hills, and orchards were painted on it. It stretched away for miles on either side.

"Why, it's nothing but scenery!"

A dozen little men in blue overalls grabbed the car and pulled it back through the hole. John was dragged screaming from the driver's seat, while a couple of the men hurriedly set to work to repair the hole in the landscape.

Mr. Brown was carried into a wooden hut and dumped in a chair. Then the door was locked.

It was a fairly normal hut. An iron stove was burning in one corner, and the walls were covered with maps and plans. A small worried-looking man with his shirt sleeves rolled up sat behind a desk groaning with paper.

"I don't know, why can't you people do what's expected of you?" moaned the worried man, shuffling through the paper. "Let's see, now—you're John Brown, off on holiday. Why didn't you stick to the main roads? We've done the scenery for that. No one was expected down this lane for years."

"Scenery—?"

"You don't think all these trees and hills just grew, did you? You're the first person to come down the lane for six months. Good heavens, think of the maintenance if we had to keep real landscape going all that time! My name's Snigsley, by the way. I'm the props manager for this stage."

There was a furious banging at the door, and Snigsley opened it to see a workman.

"Yellow alert, sir! The vicar at St. Not's has gone for a walk up to Hangman's Wood!"

"Well, that's all right."

"No, sir. 'Cos, don't you remember, we took down the Hangman's Wood scenery and painted a buttercup field on the back—there's nothing there!"

Snigsley grabbed his cap.

"Come on, this is an emergency—he'll walk backstage unless we do something!"

Snigsley, the props manager, dashed out of the hut, with John Brown in tow. A lorry pulled up. It was full of little men in blue overalls. Snigsley pushed Brown aboard and leapt on as the vehicle shot away.

"It's like this," he said, as they rushed past piles of studio lights and old scenery. "There is so much scenery that people never get close to, so really, it's much cheaper to paint it and shift it around. Take a forest. People mostly only walk through it on the paths, and only look at the trees near them. The others we make out of cardboard. There hasn't been really what you might call natural scenery in this country for about two hundred years."

"But why?" asked Brown, goggling as they drove past a neat stack of cardboard hills.

"Well, they wanted an economy drive. Only use the least amount of scenery, they said. So we have to work our fingers to the bone shifting all the trees and mountains and plastic sheep and hedges and balsa-wood fences around so that none of you actors notices a big hole in the landscape."

"Actors? I'm not an actor—I'm a chartered accountant!"

"That's right, that's your part. You act being a chartered accountant, and now something's gone wrong and you're backstage. It was the prompter's fault, probably. How do they expect us to work efficiently with the stuff they give us?"

"Who are 'They'? If I'm an actor, what's the play?"

"'They' are—the management. And the play is *The Absolute and Complete History of Earth, in 3,982,611,037,278,901,777,690,535, 016,152 Acts (and a fifteen-minute interval).*"

The lorry pulled up with a screech, and the sceneshifters piled out. Snigsley moaned and picked up a megaphone.

"The parson should be in the vicarage, not taking a walk! The scriptwriters have slipped up again. Okay, boys, grab them trees! One, two—that's right! Clompers, you sprinkle some dead leaves around—faster, man, that's it. Okay, now ferns, ferns where—FERNS. Right, birdsong, switch on the birdsong—more fungus over there, Blimpo—path, quick, puddles. Okay, get those flowers growing, bring in a few bees. BEES. Man, put that squirrel in that tree, okay, right, fine, marvelous—BEAT IT! Here he comes!"

While Brown watched in amazement the bare backstage plain was covered in earth. Trees appeared, grass sprang up, birds started to sing, and the parson ambled past, smiling pleasantly. He didn't appear to notice anything wrong. Immediately behind him the scenery was disappearing again.

Snigsley took out a red handkerchief and mopped his brow.

"That was close! One day someone's going to turn a corner and find nothing but a couple of stagehands having their tea. Right, boys, let's get back."

"What about me?" said Brown.

"You? Oh, you'll have to be written back into the play. You'll have to have a word with the scriptwriters. Go through that door over there." He pointed to a door standing all by itself in the middle of the plain.

"It doesn't lead to anywhere; I can see behind it."

"Have it your own way," said Snigsley. "I'm just Jimmy Muggins around here. You run along and don't bother me, that's all."

Brown walked around the doorway once or twice, and then decided that it was worth trying. He pushed it open, there was a flash of light and he was standing in a corridor. It was painted in brown and cream, stretched away into the distance, and was lined with doors. He peered at the untidy notice scrawled on one of them.

"Scriptwriters: Corridor 1, Room 1. Oh well, here goes."

"All right, come in."

Brown saw a small man sitting behind a typewriter. The room was full of tobacco smoke and sheets of paper were lying in drifts on the floor.

"Please, I want to get back into the play . . ." began Brown.

"What's your name—Brown? Speak up man, don't mumble! You're in the wrong corridor—go to the end and turn left. The man's an idiot, an idiot—"

Brown closed the door quietly and set off up the corridor. Several hours later he turned left into another one and after several more hours he came to a door with his name on it. In fact, there were 8,979 doors all with the same name, but before another day had passed he was level with the one that said:

"John Trevor Brown, aged 29, Chartered Accountant. 12 Windmill Place, Blackbury. Scriptwriters: Parsnip, Bagel, and Blintz."

"I'm blowed if I'm going to knock!" he thought, pushing the door open.

Parsnip, Bagel, and Blintz were standing around a typewriter with their backs to Brown. They were laughing and Bagel was slowly tapping at the typewriter.

"Right, so we've got him on the beach," he was saying. "How's about his trousers falling down? Or couldn't we get his deckchair to collapse?"

"Get him to buy an ice cream, then drop it in the sand," suggested Parsnip.

"Hey, that's good; that's very funny," said Blintz.

"Ahem," said Brown. They all turned round.

"Who are you?" said Bagel.

"I'm the man whose name is on the door," said Brown, "and you are my scriptwriters, I suppose . . ."

Blintz rushed forward and shook his hand.

"I've always wanted to meet you," he said. "You know, I've been writing your life for years, Mr. Brown. Well, I never. But how did you get here?"

"I sort of got behind the scenery," said Brown. "I was going off on holiday at the time. Is that what you were writing? I can't say I like the sound of it!"

"Oh, it's real funny," said Bagel, "a barrel of laughs. You're a natural comedian, though we say it ourselves. The audience really loves you."

"But there's billions of people in the world! How'd they see *me*?"

"They do, that's all," said Parsnip hurriedly. "Well, well, who'd have thought it? Fancy an actor coming backstage!"

"I'm not happy about my part: it's hardly a starring role," said Brown, who was getting quite used to the idea.

"Nonsense, it's a first-class piece of character acting," said Parsnip. A small green telephone, half hidden under a heap of paper, rang. He picked it up and his face went white.

"Yessir. He's here, sir. Yes, sir, I understand, sir. We'll send him right up, sir. Goodbye, sir."

"It's the Director," he said. "He wants to see you in his office. My word, you're probably in for k— You'll be lucky if you don't get the sack!"

"I'd like to see him try!" said Brown. "I've had enough, I want to go back!"

"Goodbye!" chorused the scriptwriters. There was a blue flash, a little clap of thunder and he was tumbling over and over on a very thick, red carpet.

He staggered to his feet and found that the carpet came up to his ankles. He was in an office, but the walls were so far away that they were misty. There was a large desk about half a mile away and he started to struggle towards it.

A large man in a blue suit was sitting with his feet up on the desk. He was smoking a cigar and wearing dark glasses, and when Brown approached, he was reading a newspaper.

Brown stood by the desk for five minutes, and then pointedly coughed.

"Oh, it's you, is it?" said the Director, peering over the paper. "Have a cigar? I can't understand you actors. Troublemakers, the lot of you. What's all this about?"

Brown told him his story.

"Through the scenery, eh? Oh well, it wasn't your fault. The question is, though, Brown, the question is: what shall we do with you now?"

"Look," said John Brown. "All I want is to be back in my little car. Stuck in the middle of that traffic jam. I just want to forget all about this."

The Director puffed at his cigar.

"Okay," he said. "It'll mean rewriting the plot a little bit. *Abracabazomah!*"

There was another blue flash, and Brown found himself standing by the Director on a high platform overlooking the biggest room he had ever seen. It stretched away on all sides and was full of giant bookshelves. Thousands of little men were crawling over them, and narrow-gauge electric trains were shuttling between the massive shelves, laden with volumes.

The Director beamed. "Look at this lot," he said. "Every word anybody ever said, is saying, or will say is down here somewhere—right from the first word, when a large hairy caveman dropped a log on his toe, to the last words, which I can't tell you without giving the plot away." He picked up a megaphone.

"ATTENTION! THIS IS YOUR DIRECTOR SPEAKING! BRING ME THE SCRIPT FOR CHARACTER NO. 40,908,775,821,001!"

A librarian bustled up, towing a large cart behind him. The Director lifted out a large, rather tatty book, with a red bookmark about a third of the way through it.

"Hmm, here we are. If we arrange for you to be in your car

just before you turned down that lane, it should be all right. Yes, what is it?"

A stagehand had come up and bowed respectfully. "The Producer is on the telephone for you, sir," he said.

"Won't be a moment," said the Director, hurrying away. As soon as his back was turned Brown opened the book.

He read the story of his life right up to where he entered the script room with the Director. Even as he read, the words "Brown leaps to book, begins to read" wrote themselves across the next blank page.

"Right, let's see if we can't do a bit better," he thought, and picked up a pen. Writing hurriedly, he arranged for himself to win the football pools, discover a sunken treasure galleon, win every event in the Olympic Games and die peacefully aged 198.

"This is too easy," he thought, and then an idea struck him, and a wicked smile spread across his face. Carefully he wrote: "While in the Script Room, Brown receives the scripts of the Prime Minister, the President of the United States, every other leading statesman, and Mr. Fitzburrow Robinson, chief clerk at Trouser, Trouser, Middling and Fedge, the firm where Brown at present works."

Twenty large books appeared beside him. He made a quick note in each one and just had time to write them back into their shelves before the Director hurried back.

"It's all arranged," he said. "*Blazonkeraba!*"

Brown found himself driving his car, in the middle of the traffic.

The car radio was on and the newsreader was saying: "This

morning leading politicians around the world started jumping up and down shouting, 'Long live Mr. John Brown, a marvelous chappie.' A Gritshire chief clerk also did this. There appears to be no explanation . . ."

Brown grinned. "That's upset things," he said. "Hooray!"

Pilgarlic Towers

High up in the gloomy Even Hills, in the dampest and grayest corner of Gritshire, stood the crumbling ruin known as Pilgarlic Towers.

Ivy grew on the walls, and moss grew on the ivy, and ghastly yellow toadstools grew on everything.

It was so eerie at night that even the bats avoided it, and owls used to hoot nervously under their breath.

One day a man cycled nervously up to the rusty iron gates and hung a little notice on them before hurrying away again. The notice said:

TOWN AND COUNTRY NUISANCES ACT, 1871
This property, known as Pilgarlic Towers, being subject to
sub-section 83B/a2 (1877) (as amended) of the said Act,
is going to be pulled down to make way for a motorway.
And not before time.
*By Order, Gritshire County Council, who are having their
arms twisted over this by the Ministry of Nuisances*

That night, a glowing white hand reached through the gates and grabbed the notice. Within the hour there was a riotous meeting in the drafty hall of the haunted house as all the ghosts gathered.

"Bones and rattles! This is monstrous!" said Sir Rufus Grue, the Headless Terror.

"I've lived here man and ghost for three hundred years, and now they want to turn me out," moaned the Screaming Monk. A ghostly tear rolled down his cheek.

"Well, if yer wanna know wot I fink, I fink we're due for the chop," said Cedric, the Mad Executioner.

". . . I mean, all I've ever asked for is a nice damp cellar and a bit of chain to rattle . . ." went on the Screaming Monk, sobbing.

"It's no good crying. What are we going to do?" said Lady Jane Black, offering the Monk the corner of her ghostly robe as a handkerchief.

Sir Rufus Grue tucked his head more comfortably under one arm. "What is a motorway?" he asked.

"I know," said Ronald Fitzgibbon, the Spectral Coachman who drove the phantom stagecoach around the grounds every fortnight. "It's a sort of big road for horseless carriages."

". . . just a little cellar, with a few spiders perhaps . . ." wept the Monk, blowing his nose noisily.

Sir Rufus ignored him. "I suppose we couldn't haunt this motorway?" he asked.

"No pedestrians are allowed," said Ronald. "Anyway, the drivers go so fast, they wouldn't notice anything."

". . . and a few toads to make it homely . . ." sniveled the Monk.

Sir Rufus looked thoughtful. "I have an idea," he said. "I think we'll have a little trip to London. If the Ministry of Nuisances wants to pull down our home, then they ought to provide us with another."

A week later, villagers in Pilgarlic Parva trembled in their beds as the phantom stagecoach rattled down the deserted streets.

The ghosts were all aboard, except for Septimus the Dreadful Black Dog, who ran behind it, barking. They were singing "On Ilkla Moor Baht 'At" with gusto, and a heap of ghostly luggage was strapped to the roof.

Ragged clouds scuttled over the moon as the coach swung out onto the main road in a shower of sparks. Blue flames hissed and crackled around it.

"Are you sure you know the way to London?" shouted Sir Rufus.

"Sure, and didn't I used to live there?" replied Ronald.

Lady Jane Black leaned out of a window. "There appears to be some sort of horseless carriage pursuing us. It has a flashing blue light atop it," she said.

"Crikey! Bow Street Runners!" cried Ronald, cracking his whip.

The police car chased the coach for miles, until in desperation Ronald drove right through a hedge, a haystack, five cows, a lamp post, two cottages, and an orchard. Of course, the coach, being ghostly, passed through them all like a puff of mist.

The eastern sky was pink as the coach entered London. The ghosts were all craning their necks for a good view.

"Westminster! Ah, how it brings back memories!" said Sir Rufus. "Did you know I was once MP for Blackbury? Of course, that was in the good old days, before they gave the vote to the common riff-raff."

The phantom stagecoach drew up outside the Ministry of Nuisances, and the ghosts swarmed out and through the revolving doors.

The building was very new. Sir Rufus shuddered to see how neat and clean everything was. There wasn't a decent cobweb in sight.

"Doesn't seem to be anyone about," he said.

Lady Jane Black looked around. "I expect they only have a skeleton staff here at this time of a morning," she said.

"Ah! Now, that's more like it," said the ghostly knight.

"I mean there's only a few people."

"Oh."

By now the ghosts were wandering all over the Ministry.

Cedric the Mad Executioner gave himself a nasty shock on an electric typewriter.

The Monk caught his finger in a filing cabinet, and burst into tears.

Ronald Fitzgibbon, who was interested in mechanical things, was investigating a large computer, which had five rooms all to itself.

Sir Rufus strode along the shiny corridors until he found an impressive door marked:

RT. HON. RICHARD CARPET,
MINISTER FOR NUISANCES

"The very man!" he thought, and entered through the keyhole.

He had a long wait. But finally, around half past ten, a slightly pompous-looking man entered and sat down at a huge shiny desk.

Sir Rufus tucked his head under his arm and rose majestically out of the inkwell.

"OOOOOoooooH!" he moaned. "The hour of doom steals darkly o'er the ghastly sands!"

The Minister leaned over to his intercom and said calmly, "Bring me the file on Bothers please, Miss Fisher."

Sir Rufus had a feeling that something was wrong. He tried again.

"AAAAAaaaaah! Tremble, ye mortal!"

The Minister lit his pipe and stared out of the window.

"It's no good, he can't see you or hear you," said Lady Jane Black, materializing on the windowsill. "I've just spent ten minutes haunting Miss Fisher, his secretary. She didn't notice a thing."

Cedric the Mad Executioner stepped out of the wall. He looked really magnificent, and glowed green. "It's no good, they don't believe in us," he said.

"This is monstrous," said Sir Rufus, bristling. "In the good old days we used to terrorize the country for miles around."

"Yes, but people expected ghosts. These days we're just ridiculous superstition. Anyway, how can you haunt a building like this," muttered Lady Jane Black.

"Look!" said Sir Rufus.

The Minister was reading a long official-looking document headed "Pilgarlic Towers Demolition Order."

"We must do something! Surely there's some way we can get through!"

The intercom buzzed, and said: "I'm very sorry to bother you, sir, but—er—well, the computer has gone wrong."

"I don't see why that should cause you to bother me, Miss Fisher."

"Yes, sir, but, well it's singing dirty songs, sir."

"Good grief!" said the Minister, and rushed from the room.

"It's Ronald!" cried the ghosts.

"He's found a way! He's haunting the computer!" said Sir Rufus.

In the room below, the machine, having typed out a very questionable ballad entitled "As Turpin Was A'Riding," was telling an eighteenth-century joke.

As soon as the ghosts got the hang of things the Ministry came to a halt. Filing cabinets refused to budge. Lifts flew up and down. One, containing no less a person than the Secretary for Official Nosiness, yo-yo'ed between the basement and the eighth floor nineteen times before kicking him out on the roof.

The Minister was hurrying down the fire escape when a telephone shot out of a window and lassoed him in its cord. He was dragged onto the tea trolley which carried him, white with fear, down to the computer.

It typed: NO OFFENSE MEANT, BUT THIS SORT OF THING WILL CONTINUE UNLESS YOU PREVENT PILGARLIC TOWERS FROM BEING PULLED DOWN.

"I can't!" he gasped. "The bulldozers are already there!"

A telephone drifted over, and the computer typed: TELL THEM TO STOP WORK.

Trembling, the Minister did so. And, like magic, the Ministry went back to normal.

Later, of course, he decided it had all been due to overwork or something. But when two bulldozers, sent back to work, turned on each other and started butting like rams, he looked thoughtful.

Suddenly it was discovered that Pilgarlic Towers was of great historical interest, and the motorway had to go around it.

The ghosts were pleased to have their home back, but they had grown slightly bored with ordinary haunting.

So, when telephones ring for no reason and computers go wrong, or when typewriters suddenly seem to have a mind of their own, it's probably just Sir Rufus or the Screaming Monk having a bit of fun.

The Quest for the Keys

Far away and long ago, when dragons still existed and the only arcade game was ping-pong in black and white, a wizard cautiously entered a smoky tavern in the evil, ancient, foggy city of Morpork and sidled up to the bar.

Wizards aren't generally welcome in pubs. They tend to score one hundred and ninety at darts.

"I'm looking for a hired sword," this one said to the innkeeper.

"Ah?" said the innkeeper. "Someone who can brave unimaginable terrors, fight nameless monsters, the usual stuff?"

"The very same, yes," said the wizard.

"The bloke in the corner might be your man."

The wizard looked around. Sitting on a bench by the fire was a young man with the shoulders of an ox, an honest face, and the sort of impractical leather clothes that no true adventurer would be seen dead out of.

"Reckon he's tough, then?" said the wizard.

"Well, he's just eaten fifteen bags of pork scratchings, a bucket of cheese 'n' smoky dragon-flavored crisps, ten pickled eggs and an old individual meat pie I was using as a paperweight," said the innkeeper.

"Good grief," said the wizard. "Then just give me a pint of inexpensive ale and a small lemonade with a cherry in it, please."

"I won't beat about the bush," he said, sitting down next to the big man. "My name is Grubble the Utterly Untrustworthy, and I'm looking for a hero."

The man extended a hand like a bunch of bananas.

"That's me," he said. "I'm called Kron." His mighty brows furrowed, and his lips moved silently. "Yah, I'm sure that's right," he said uncertainly. "Yah, Kron."

"Well, Kron, I just happen to have found out the whereabouts of the Five Keys of Zag—what do you think of that, then?"

Kron's expression did not change. "I expect that's very nice for you," he said.

"Nononono," said Grubble sharply. "You don't say that, you say 'Not the Five Keys of Zag, whose fabulous treasure has been seen by no man for a thousand years, gosh, how marvelous, let me help you in your quest, O wizard, in exchange for not more than twenty per cent of the treasure less expenses, when do I start?'"

"Hokay," said Kron. "I wasn't doing much today anyway."

"We'll have to hurry," said Grubble. "The first one shouldn't be too tricky. It's kept by an old witch who can only do food spells—should be, heheh, a piece of cake."

"Seems fair enough," said Kron. "When do I start—"

"GONDROPISTREL!" shouted the wizard. Kron vanished so suddenly that there was a small thunderclap.

"Can't let him ask too many questions," said Grubble to

himself, as he hurried from the inn. "He'll just have to do what he's best at and I'll do what I'm best at, which will probably involve swindling him out of his share of the treasure if he ever finds it. Shouldn't be too difficult—he seems a bit lightweight in the head department."

"Hang on," said Kron. "There's one or two questions I'd like—"

He was alone, in the middle of a forest. And it was immediately obvious that it was the sort of forest where even the monsters went around in pairs, for safety: huge, gnarled, and sinister-looking trees loomed off in all directions.

If there was a map of the forest it would have been entirely green, with a little dot right in the middle of it and an arrow telling Kron: *You Are Here. But Not For Very Long, Probably.*

He drew his sword and looked around carefully. At about that moment, someone shouted "Duck!"

Now, in a situation like that the average person does the obvious thing, i.e., stand still with their mouth open, looking gormless. But Kron tumbled forward just as a spear whistled over his head and stuck, vibrating like a tuning fork, in a tree. Something cackled and disappeared among the bushes.

"What was that?" said Kron out loud.

"Well, that depends what you mean by 'that,'" said a voice by his ear. It was a rather wooden, hollow voice. It went on: "By the way, would you mind taking this spear out of me?"

Kron looked up into a large oak tree. What was more unusual was that the oak tree looked back.

"You're a tree?" said Kron.

The tree groaned.

"Yes," it said. "Some people would say that the roots, branches, general bark-like covering and of course all these leaves all over the place are a dead giveaway but yes, since you ask, I am a tree. Did Grubble send you?"

"How did you know that?"

The tree shrugged, which was quite an impressive sight.

"Another idiot treasure hunter," it said. "That makes three this week. It doesn't work, you know. The witch knows where he materializes them, and just waits here and spears them or puts a spell on them or whatever."

"He never said anything about that," said Kron.

"He wouldn't, would he," said the tree. "I mean, saying 'Step this way, certain death guaranteed' doesn't attract volunteers, does it?"

Kron looked at the spear.

"I've survived so far," he said. "Where does this witch live?"

"About a mile away," said the tree. "I'll help you get there, if you want."

"Sure," said Kron. A branch creaked down towards him.

"Hop on," said the tree.

It was a jerky way to travel, but fast. The oak tree swung round slowly and dropped Kron gently into the waiting branches of a nearby ash tree, which passed him on to a handy beech. The ground swayed and moved a long way below him.

"Be careful," said a chestnut tree, as it handed him on. "The witch has got this dog, you see . . ."

The witch certainly did have a dog.* It had two heads and was almost as tall as Kron.

---

* She obviously hadn't heard that she ought to have a cat.

He'd have to do something about it if he wanted to get to the witch's cottage, which was quite unlike anything he'd ever seen before. A few bones and odd bits of armor around the clearing suggested that other people had also tried. The dog didn't look very friendly. It did look hungry.

Kron, from a handy bush, watched it for a while and looked at his spear. It didn't look anything like enough to . . .

He had an idea.

The assembled trees watched in horror as Kron stepped out from the bush, snapped the spear across his knee, and stood grinning with half a spear in either hand.

"He's gone totally mad," muttered a holly bush.

"Here boy," called Kron.

The two-headed dog wasn't used to this sort of thing. It came across the clearing at a lumbering run, both heads dribbling horribly and straining to be the first one to bite him.

Then Kron threw the spear away.

"Mad," said a beech tree. "Doomed, too."

The two-headed dog thundered towards Kron. So, he threw the two halves of his spear in opposite directions and shouted "Fetch!"

There was a long moment as the dog hung in the air with its heads trying to take the body after each bit of spear. Then the heads snapped back, knocked into each other, and the dog rolled over—out cold.

Kron scampered towards the witch's cottage, and flung himself against a wall. Which was made of gingerbread.

The whole place was made of gingerbread. Here and there, of course, whoever had built it had to use other things—like, for example, all sorts of licorice on the chimney and the chocolate doorsteps—but by and large it was certainly gingerbread.

There was a candyfloss doorknocker, and the doorhandle felt sticky. Toffee, Kron realized. He couldn't let go. And the door was opening.

"The toffee doorknob trick gets them every time!" cackled the witch, herding Kron into her kitchen. "That ratbag old wizard never gives up!"

Kron's arms were pinned to his side by a very large doughnut.

The kitchen was big and smelled rather sweet, as might be expected in a cottage belonging to a witch who could only do high-carbohydrate spells. There were several cages against one wall, and Kron was pushed into one of them.

"They say I should move with the times," the witch muttered. "They say I should do this place up, get rid of all the sweet stuff, do the whole thing over with brown bread and yogurt—as if anyone ever heard of a wholefood cottage."

"Yeah, ridiculous," agreed Kron.

"I don't know, you rot people's teeth, steal their kids, make them all spotty and then suddenly they turn against you for no reason at all," said the witch. "You're a big lad, anyway. Couple of weeks' eating on you, I shouldn't wonder, after you've been fattened up a bit."

"You eat people?" said Kron.

"It's traditional," said the witch. "It goes with the job."

She hobbled out of the room, leaving Kron to look around. There was a key hanging over the—*gulp*—big oven. The key of Zag? There was also a very small and ugly troll in the next cage.

"Hi, man," said the troll, wearily.

"Been here long?" said Kron.

"Ages, man," said the troll. "Don't seem to put on weight. If she'd feed me decent slugs or toads it'd be fine, but I can't stand all this sweet stuff. I'd eat my way out of here tomorrow if I could abide the taste of licorice."

Kron looked at the cage bars. They were thick and black, he already knew. But they were also sticky. With every muscle twanging like an elastic band Kron broke free of his doughnut and attacked the licorice bars with his teeth. The troll watched with interest.

By the time the witch came back Kron had eaten through three bars and was feeling sick. She gave a screech, but even as she waved a hand and materialized a mass of marshmallow over his head he squeezed forward and was free.

"Hey, man," said the troll. "Don't forget me; the old complexion isn't getting any better here!"

At that moment the gingerbread door burst in, and the witch's two-headed dog leapt at Kron, both heads growling. He hit it as hard as he could, grabbed his sword from the table, cut through several of the troll's bars, snatched the key from its hook, and ducked as the witch sent a stream of razor-sharp barley sugars scything through the air.

"Hey, wow, dog!" said the troll, squeezing out of its cage. "Anybody got any mustard?"

The monster dog bit it on both legs which, since troll skin is tougher than leather, wasn't a particularly good idea. The troll bit back. A second later both were gone, with the sounds of distant yelping and the troll shouting for salt and pepper.

The witch had gone, too. Kron kicked his way through a wall, in time to see her broomstick hurtling away over the trees.

Kron held the key over his head. "Okay, Grubble," he said. "I've got the key. Do your stuff."

He vanished.

Kron winked into existence in the middle of a pile of what felt like . . . cardboard boxes. He pushed at them and heard Grubble's muffled voice:

"Oi! That's quality merchandise!"

Light streamed in as the wizard moved some of the boxes out of the way and helped Kron climb out. He was in a cave which had a few motheaten magical implements in it but was mostly full of cardboard boxes.

"Got the key?" said Grubble, and snatched it out of Kron's hand. "Fine, great, super. Now your next quest, I want you to—"

"Hang on," said Kron quickly. "We ought to have a talk."

"No time," said Grubble. "I've got to shift all this lot."

Kron looked at the boxes. "What are they?"

"Lucky charms," said Grubble. "Got them cheap on account of the manufacturer being struck by lightning. Real bargains, genuine solid brass plating, only three gold pieces each to you, all right, two, okay, one—but I'm cutting my own throat. Tell you what I'll do, tell you what I'll do. I'll throw in one totally genuine love potion with every three charms sold. Can't say fairer than that, can I?"

"You just did," said Kron.

"All this magic to move you around is costing me a packet,"

moaned the wizard. "Come on, buy a couple, they're only slightly tarnished where they were in the mystery flood that happened after the fire. You'd hardly notice."

"No," said Kron. "Look, I'm not all that happy about these quests; it looks like I'm taking a lot of risks."

"Hardly any," said Grubble. "Not worth talking about, really. Now, if you'll just stand in this magic circle here . . ."

"Yes," said Kron, who was beginning to think he'd lost a grip on the conversation. "But—"

"SWERSGROMMLE!" said Grubble.

Kron vanished.

There were one or two things about Kron that the wizard ought to have found out. While Kron was quite bright for a hero, he couldn't tell north from south and always got them confused. He was okay with east and west, and up and down didn't give him a lot of trouble either.

He zapped into existence in broad daylight in a rocky landscape, which was freezing cold even though steam gushed up from holes in the ground.

"That wasn't very polite," he said. "Still, now I'm here I'd better have a look round. Let's see, there's a cave behind me—due south—and that's a big volcano up there. I think I'll take a look at that funny stone near it."

It was a tall rock with the mystifying words IT SNORT HO'ME carved on it.

"Who or what is 'it snort ho'me'?" Kron said out loud.

There was a groan from behind the rock. Drawing his sword, Kron went to investigate.

On the ground, totally tied up, was a very small man. "Help, help," the little man suggested.

"Hold on a moment," said Kron, and took out his *Adventurers' Pocket Guide to Mythical Creatures*.

"Hmm," he said. "Very small, got a beard—could be a goblin? No, wrong color hat. Dwarf? That's interesting, it says here that dwarfs always tell lies in the afternoon and hate personal remarks. Elf? No, beard's too long—"

"When you've quite finished," said the little man. "I'm a gnome. Set me free and I'll tell you what the rock means."

"Well?" said Kron, after he had untied the gnome.

"It points the way if you read it right," said the little man. "The dwarfs put it here as a marker. They also attacked me and tied me up because they thought I was looking for one of the keys, which they have hidden."

"Were you?"

"Who, me?" said the gnome, guiltily. "All I know about it is that it is not under ice, whatever that means."

Kron hurried off down the road, and the gnome watched him go south.

When Kron came to a fork in the road, he tossed a coin to decide which way to go. Then he ran across a bridge but did not take the next turning, which he could see led to a steaming lake. At the next turning he headed for a very rickety bridge— where there was a small black book.

When Kron picked up the book, it said: "If you think you're heading west, then I'll tell you the key isn't on land. If you think you're heading east, then I'll tell you the key isn't in the water. If you think you're going north of the Pointy Hills, then I'll tell you the key is west of the Pointy Hills. And shall I tell you something for nothing?"

"What's that?" said Kron.

"You've got mud all over your boots."

Kron looked down. His boots were filthy.

"Fifty gold pieces a pair, these cost me," he moaned. "You just can't get mud off Hush Dragons."

But he sat down on a nearby rock to try. This turned out to be the wrong thing to do for two reasons. One, he caught a slight chill from the cold stone; and two, the party of dwarfs that had been watching him from behind the rock took the opportunity to hit him very hard indeed.

When Kron woke up, he was heavily bound with dwarf ropes and lying in one of the many caves that riddled the hills in the area. He could see dwarfish writing on the walls. "This must be their camp," he thought.

He also noticed about seventeen other things. Sixteen of them were dwarfs, none of them more than two feet high. The other was a very ornate clock, which the dwarfs were watching carefully.

The hands were pointing to one minute to twelve.

"Oh dear," said Kron loudly. "This is going to be very embarrassing."

"He's woked up!" shouted a dwarf.

"The reason it's going to be embarrassing," said Kron, standing up and snapping all the ropes, "is that dwarfs make very bad ropes, but if it gets about that I fought a lot of dwarfs I'll get laughed out of the Heroes' Union."

"Oh, why?" said the head dwarf.

"Well," said Kron. "You've got to admit you're all a bit lacking in the inches department."

"Get him, lads!" shouted the head dwarf. "Nut him in the kneecaps!"

Kron ignored the little men who were kicking him on the ankle but managed to pick up the head dwarf by his belt and held him at arm's length while he struggled.

"I don't normally attack people smaller than me," he said. "But I'll make an exception in your case unless you tell me where you've hidden the key."

"I'll tell you two things," said the dwarf, sulkily. "The key is in a cave . . ."

"Bong!" said the clock, twelve times, and Kron said: "Fancy that—it's the afternoon already."

"And it is east of the Six Standing Stones," finished the dwarf triumphantly.

Kron thought for a moment.

"I don't need to know any more," he said, "I know where the key is!"

As soon as Kron laid hands on the second key of Zag, Grubble the wizard's magic took hold and flipped him back to the cave. At least, Kron hoped it was the cave . . .

All the cardboard boxes had gone. But there was a lot of glass pipework, and bubbling jars, and steam. Nasty-colored liquids jerked along corkscrew pipes and dripped into bottles. And at the end of it all, Grubble the Utterly Untrustworthy was sitting with a pile of sticky labels and a funnel.

"What happened to the lucky charm business?" said Kron.

"Traded them with Scrobblast the Devious for all this stuff," said the wizard, licking a label and sticking it onto a full bottle of horrible blue stuff.

"What are you making, then?"

"Magic potions," said the wizard, pointing to half a dozen crates of bottles, all corked and labeled.

'What sort?'

"Well," said Grubble, pointing to the stack of labels. "What sort would you like?"

Kron picked up a handful of labels. "What's this?" he said. "'Love potion,' 'Strength potion,' 'Anti-Welsh-television ointment,' 'Flying potion' . . . all on the same stuff? And it says here 'Guaranteed one hundred per cent artificial additives' . . . It's just a load of rubbish, how can you call it magic?"

"Absolutely true description," said Grubble shiftily. "People are paying five gold pieces a bottle for stuff like this, and if that isn't magic, I don't know what is. Got the key, have you?"

Kron handed it over reluctantly.

"These adventures," he began. "They're a bit risky, and I want to have a talk about how much I'm going to be pa—"

"What, you don't trust me?" said Grubble. "That's shocking, that is."

"It's not that I don't actually trust you," said Kron. "It's more that I sort of, well, don't trust you at all, to tell the truth."

"THREEPSNANCE!" shouted the wizard. Kron vanished.

Grubble looked at the two keys. "Three to go," he muttered. "And then I'll be as rich as Creosote."

Kron reappeared standing on a narrow, ice-covered ledge several thousand feet up a sheer cliff, during a blizzard.

"Oh, great," he muttered. "Really first class. Marvelous. How am I supposed to get out of this?"

He tried not to look down, and sidled along the ledge which, just to make things interesting, slanted outwards from the cliff and was getting covered with wet, slippery snow. Icy water began to trickle down his neck.

"I say, I say, I say, excuse please," said a voice behind him. Kron turned his head gingerly and saw a very small bald man standing on the ledge. He wore a black robe and was barefoot, but what was more surprising was that he had a large red rubber nose, attached to his face by elastic knotted around his ears.

In fact, this is standard dress for a Joke Monk, but Kron wasn't to know that.

"Excuse please, boomboom, kindly leave the ledge," said the monk, in a singsong voice. "I say, I say."

"You must be joking," said Kron weakly.

"Yes, must be joking, so please to stand aside, boomboom," said the monk.

When Kron stayed put, the monk shrugged, walked around him so easily that Kron was sure the little man had taken several steps on empty air, and ran along the ledge.

Kron swallowed. "Well, if he can do that, so can I," he thought. But he didn't believe himself.

By the time Kron reached the end of the ledge, the blizzard had stopped and the sun was out. He could see high mountains covered with snow, and gleaming glaciers stretching into the distance. Since they were nearly all a long way below him, this was no great help.

The joke monk was a distant dot on a wide snowfield that

was cupped in a hollow of the mountain. Kron followed him as best he could, sinking knee deep in the snow at every step.

Finally, the monk disappeared between two tall rocks. When Kron reached them, he found himself looking down—into a narrow valley, full of gardens and trees, hidden from the outside world by the high mountains.

The little monk was talking to two guards who blocked the path. They were so big and muscular their arms looked like two sacks of melons.

"My dog got no nose," the little monk chanted.

"How he smell?" asked one of the guards.

"Terrible, boomboom," said the little monk.

"Do not wish to know that, kindly go on down path," said the guard, standing aside.

"Jokes?" muttered Kron, who was hiding behind one of the rocks. "They live up here and tell JOKES?"

Well, anything was better than freezing to death. He stepped out and walked up to the guards, who barred his way with their spears.

And he tried to think of a joke.

"Um," said Kron. The two guards watched him.

"What do you call a dog that is magic?" he said.

"What you call him?" said one of the guards.

"A Labracadabrador," said Kron, nervously. "Boomboom."

The guards looked at each other.

"All right," said Kron. "Do you know the one about the man who made a run for it?"

"How that go?" said a guard.

"Like this," said Kron.

He sped on down the zigzag path until the surprised guards were left far behind and, when he stopped for breath, he could see the whole valley spread out in front of him. There were little monks tending the gardens and herding goats, and every monk had a large red rubber nose held on with elastic.

Even the big monastery at the head of the valley had a large red round roof.

Finally, Kron caught up with the monk he was following. "Where is this place?" he asked.

The little monk grinned at him.

"This place Lost Valley of Shangri Larf, boomboom. You come be joke monk, all day long tell joke, become big monk like Alec Guinness only not so well paid?"

"Actually, I was looking for the key—" Kron began.

The little monk grabbed his arm. "You come see High Lama," he said firmly. "Boomboom."

Kron was led into the monastery and into the presence of the High Lama, who sat on possibly the only throne in the world with a built-in whoopee cushion.

He wore a fez and, in addition to the red nose that all the monks had, also wore a pair of plastic spectacles with false eyebrows.

"Here in Shangri Larf we find amazing secret of living for long time," said the Lama. "For example, I am two hundred years old.

"We tell jokes all day, everyone keep happy, live long time," continued the Lama. "Also, prophecy say when all jokes in world been told nine billion times, whole world come to end, just like that, and everyone allowed to go home."

"That's fine by me," said Kron. "But I was actually looking for the key of Zag."

"We have it in treasure house," said the Lama. "Prophecy say it be given to first man who tell us joke we haven't heard before, boomboom."

"Oh, I expect I can do that," said Kron.

"Good," said the Lama. "Because prophecy also say—well, you know when comic on stage, he tell joke and audience no like, he is said to 'die'? Where you come from is just figure of speech. Up here, joke no make us laugh, we don't mess about. Boomboom."

Kron suddenly became very aware of all the guards in the hall. They all wore red noses, but the spears and swords they carried were no laughing matter.

"Er, when you say you don't mess about," he said, "what do you mean?"

"Joke no make us laugh, we hit comic in face with traditional one-thousand-year-old custard pie . . ."

"That's a relief!"

". . . then we throw him off cliff and have good laugh."

Kron was led into a little room deep in the heart of the monastery, where one of the monks was waiting for him, holding out a red nose.

"Stranger must wear ceremonial costume," he said.

Then a gong sounded, and guards escorted both of them to a courtyard where thousands of joke monks were waiting expectantly. On a stage one monk was telling . . . jokes?

"1,456,098!" he shouted, and all the monks laughed; and "45,875,449!" he cried, and they all cheered; and "87,076!" he sniggered, and they all clapped.

"Fwhat's all this?" said Kron, muffled by the nose.

"We heard all joke so many time, easier to give each joke number," said the High Lama. "Monks hear number, think of joke, all laughing, boomboom. Efficiency."

He pushed Kron forward. "You're on!"

Kron shuffled out onto the stage and a small orchestra struck up a tune which sounded like a handful of steel bars falling down a fire escape.

The huge crowd of joke monks waited expectantly—not for the joke, probably, but to see Kron hit in the face by the ceremonial one-thousand-year-old custard pie which was being held by two guards.

"Um," said Kron. "Er . . ." The custard pie smelled really awful and had a stale crust that was razor sharp.

He thought: All jokes have numbers! "199,874,390!" he shouted.

There was silence then one monk began to snigger. Then, another moment later, the crowd was falling about with laughter.

They hadn't heard that one before.

Kron didn't waste time. He grabbed the High Lama and pulled his red rubber nose out as far as the elastic would stretch.

"Gimme the key," he growled, "or I'll fnill you fnull of nose."

"No problem," said the Lama, who was shaking with laughter. "You're welcome. Very funny joke, how you think 'em up? There is famous key of Zag and as special treat you get to eat traditional custard pie."

Kron didn't feel hungry. He grabbed the key and ran, with the guards after him.

He didn't stop at the entrance to the valley. In fact, he didn't stop when he came to the cliff.

He jumped. "Grubble, do your fstuff!" he screamed.

There was the usual blinding flash of light, and Kron found himself lying on the floor of Grubble's cave.

The wizard was working at a table covered with papers and didn't look up.

"Everything okay?" was all he said. "No problems?"

Kron tore off the rubber nose and baggy trousers. "Lots," he said, "but it isn't worth me telling you, because as soon as I complain you just say a magic word and I end up in something even worse."

He flung the third key of Zag onto the table, disturbing piles of paper covered with complicated magical calculations.

"Ta," said Grubble. "What's eight times three?"

"888," said Kron.

"Sure? It doesn't look right."

Kron peered over the wizard's shoulder. He was drawing shaky red lines on a chart covered with strange symbols.

"What's all this about?" he asked.

"The fourth key was hidden in time and space," said Grubble wearily. "Very tricky, trying to work out the magic to get you there.

"TREMBLIGHT!" said Grubble, and nothing happened. "Obviously need more bias in the nether areas," he muttered.

"TROWBLOWED!"

Purple sparks flashed out of Kron's ears. Green light flickered around his head, and he began to wobble slightly.

"Hang on, almost got it—TRIBLIFFEN!"

Kron vanished.

Grubble picked up the three keys.

"Only two to go!" he gloated. "888? Still doesn't sound right . . ."

Kron spun helplessly in space. This wasn't like the normal magic—the darkness was full of horrible noises and blinding flashes of light.

Finally, it stopped. There was a last blue flash and he was sitting in dusty darkness in something small and crowded and smelling of—what? Furniture polish? He reached out carefully and touched a wooden stick, which fell over with a clatter. Then something smooth and snakelike dropped over his neck.

With a scream Kron drew his sword and hacked madly at the blackness.

He tried to back away in the cramped space and bumped into a door which swung open. He fell through backwards, followed by a clutter of tins, brushes, old boots, and the snake monster.

He gave it a few more wallops with the sword, to make sure it was dead, and hurried down the passage into a dimly lit room that seemed to be mainly white boxes. His heart pounding, Kron pulled cautiously at the handle on the nearest one—and found the box was full of winter.

The box was freezing cold, and someone had been stupid enough to put food in it.

There was nearly a whole roast chicken, for example. Kron decided to really investigate the chicken, thoroughly.

While he chewed, he padded cautiously around the room.

There was a big black box thing with knobs on the front, and when Kron prodded at them, rings on top of the box glowed red.

There was a big metal basin with a couple of spiky things on the back of it. Kron couldn't quite see how they worked, so he hit them with the end of his sword until one broke off and sent a fountain of water spurting across the room.

Kron backed away and looked at a smaller box with more knobs on. He poked at them . . . and the room was suddenly full of noise, howling and screaming around while Kron desperately poked again at the knobs.

This just caused different sorts of noise and even the sound of people talking.

"Demons!" he thought, and "People trapped in little boxes by wizardry!"

He brought his sword down hard and the box flew apart in a shower of sparks. There weren't even any very small people inside.

And then Kron heard a voice behind him and the room was flooded with light. "Mom! Mom! There's a man with a sword in the kitchen and he's just killed the radio!"

"'Ere, you haven't half made a mess of our vacuum cleaner," said a very small boy in blue pajamas, who was standing in the doorway. "You haven't come out of a flying saucer, have you? Like in that film, you know—*bing bong bing bang BONG*."

Kron backed away hastily from the little maniac, and unfortunately put his hand down on the top of the hot stove.

"You're even uglier than E.T.," said the boy, conversationally.

"Argh!" Kron screamed, and stepped backwards into the washing machine, which started to churn and rumble.

Finally, in sheer terror, he vaulted onto the sink and dived out through the window.

He was vaguely aware of shouts behind him as he pounded across some grass and jumped a fence. But there was worse to come. For example, the street was very small, with little suns on poles, and what could only be a dragon was roaring towards him.

That was a relief, at least. Kron knew about dragons. This one was a funny shape and had two glowing eyes, but it was a dragon all right.

He stepped out in front of it and drew his sword. There was a nasty squealing noise and a roar of hot breath as the dragon slowed down—and when it was almost upon him, Kron struck.

Kron's sword hit the dragon right between its glowing eyes. It was quite effective—there was a gush of steam and the eyes went out.

A small voice behind him said: "You've done it now, killing that lorry."

Kron looked around. The little boy, who had put on a dressing gown over his pajamas, was standing on the pavement watching him with interest.

A door opened in the side of the dragon and a small but very angry man got out.

"My mom's called the police," said the little boy. "Why haven't you got green skin like the Incredible Wossname?"

The lorry driver was rolling up his sleeves. Kron's sword was stuck fast. He ran for it.

He didn't stop until he was several streets away. "Grubble," he muttered under his breath, "if I ever get out of this mad place, I'll twist your horrible head off."

Smaller dragons were roaring up and down the road. A big one flew overhead, flashing lights and growling. There were lights and noises everywhere. Kron felt lost, helpless, alone and very, very hungry . . .

Kron sniffed. There was a strange smell in the air—tangy and tasty and mouthwatering, quite unlike anything he'd ever come across.

Across the dark street he could see a sign, magically glowing. He could read it, but he couldn't understand it. It said:

FISH 'N' CHIPS TO TAKE AWAY

Kron had never heard of a fish'n'chip, but he plucked up courage and went in.

The sight of a seven-foot man wearing leather and furs and dribbling a bit rather upset the shop owner, but not a lot, because he was already far more upset by another man in the shop who was pointing a gun at him and rummaging in the till.

The man swung round and pointed the little black metal thing at Kron, who looked at it blankly. This man was trying to stop him getting at the lovely smell. Kron walloped him.

There was a cheer, and lots of people crawled out from under the tables where they had been hiding. Kron ignored them and banged on the counter.

"Fish'n'chip," he demanded.

"Better give it to him," said a little voice behind him proudly. "He's a Master of the Universe or summing."

Kron looked down, knowing what he was going to see. The little boy added: "And a cod and double chips for me, too, please."

"He can have everything he can eat," said the chip-shop man, as Kron was surrounded by customers who were standing on tiptoe trying to slap him on the back. The would-be robber was out cold.

Kron sat down and worked his way through piles of cod and plaice, a vat of mushy peas, every sausage in the place and enough chips to build a rather greasy model of St. Paul's Cathedral. The small boy in the dressing gown sat opposite him, beaming proudly. He'd obviously adopted Kron as a kind of pet.

At that moment a car with a blue flashing light stopped outside. Kron had a feeling that meant trouble—and he hadn't found the key! He couldn't go home! He could almost cry.

"I think it might be a good idea for you to go out the back way," said the little boy. "The police might not understand about the lorry." He grabbed Kron's arm.

There was a flash. There was sudden darkness. Kron found himself whirling through space—without the key!

Magical lights flickered around him, the whole universe started to flash on and off . . . and a little voice behind him said: "'Ere, is this some sort of disco?"

Kron reappeared in Grubble's cave.

The wizard was busy applying woodworm killer to a very battered broomstick.

There was a label on it which said: *"A snip! This weke's bargain! Only won owner, an old ladie who onlie took it out on Halloween!,"* in bright red lettering.

With a slightly smaller pop the small boy in the dressing

gown appeared beside Kron. The wizard stepped back so suddenly he sprayed woodworm killer all up his sleeve.

"What's that?!"

"He just followed me," Kron said miserably. "I think he's a magician, that place you sent me to was full of them, you've no idea—"

"Um," said Grubble. "Er, don't be frightened, little boy."

"I'm not," said the boy, looking around the cave. "I know all about beaming people up and stuff like that. Is this a real magician's cave?"

"Beaming people— Yes, it is," said Grubble. "You may find it a little bit scary but—"

"It smells of old socks."

"What is your name, boy?" said Grubble, his eyes narrowing. "Apart from rude little nuisance, of course."

"Alan," said the boy. "Alan Key."

Kron looked at the wizard, who shrugged.

"There's nothing to say the keys of Zag are ordinary metal keys," said Grubble thoughtfully. "They're magic, after all— they could be anything."

"Does that mean we're stuck with him?"

"'Fraid so."

"But I don't know anything about children!" wailed Kron.

"They're just people with short legs," said Grubble. "You give them milk. And, er, bicycles. You don't have to be afraid of them—PUT THAT DOWN!—and they like, er, dolls . . ."

"A complete set of Star Wars characters, please," said Alan, poking at something nasty in a jar, which blinked at him. "Doesn't anyone clean up in here?"

"I'm not going on another quest," said Kron, firmly. "I've been hit over the head, attacked by dragons, frozen, and nearly eaten by unpleasant people, and I'm going on strike. What have you got to say to that, hey?"

"Only one thing," said Grubble.

"Well?"

"SPANFROOD!"

Kron vanished. Much to the wizard's astonishment, so did Alan.

"My magic must be better than I thought," he said.

Kron flashed into existence. Imagine his surprise to find that no one was shouting at him, the weather was nice, he was in a little wood, birds were singing, and there wasn't a cloud in the sky. He wasn't even too annoyed when Alan popped into existence a few yards away.

"Do you have to do a lot of this in your job?" Alan asked.

"Too much," said Kron, bitterly.

The wood was on the top of a hill. In the valley he could see several brightly painted tents around a large gray castle, and hundreds of people were milling around.

"I suppose we'd better go and have a look," he said. "I need a sword though—I left mine in that dragon thingy."

"Lorry," corrected Alan.

"Yeah, dragon lorry," said Kron. "Come on."

There was some sort of fair going on in the valley, with stalls like roll-a-groat, bowl for an ogre, and duck witches in the moat, which was all rather boring but better than having to wait a thousand years for television to be invented.

At the center of the fair, though, was a wide clear area with a big red tent in it.

And in front of it, surrounded by a crowd of people, was a sword. Stuck in a stone.

There was a message carved in the stone. In ancient mystical letters it said:

Whosoever Pulls This Sword Out of This Stone Will Win a Spanish Holiday for Two, the Key of the Castle, Complete Double Glazing, and a Cuddly Toy.

Kron and Alan read this. Kron said: "What's double glazing?"

Alan said, "It's like extra glass in your windows."

"Oh," said Kron, and, "What's glass?"

Various beefy types were climbing up the steps to the sword and trying to pull it out, urged on by the crowd. The sword didn't budge.

An elderly magician with a pointy hat and regulation long white beard bustled up to them with a wad of forms.

"Fancy trying your luck, young sirs?" he said, handing Kron a form. "Just pull the sword, and fame and fortune would be yours, only five gold pieces to try."

"What kind of cuddly toy?" Kron asked. The sword didn't look too bad, he thought. It could be worth having, especially if the cuddly toy was a decent one.

"You get three goes," said the wizard, encouragingly.

"It's a fix," said Alan. "Have they got any video games here?" He wandered off.

Alan soon got bored with the fair. There was no electricity

and no buttons to press, and it had also started to rain. He wandered around to the back of the big red tent and peered inside.

In front of the tent, Kron was being led up to the sword in the stone by a young lady with sequined tights and the crowds were quite expectant. Kron, after all, had arms that looked like two sacksful of melons—he might even manage to win the prize.

"Oh-kay," bellowed the old wizard, through a megaphone. "The next contender is Kron the Barbarian . . . first try!"

Inside the tent several other wizards were peering through a hole.

"He looks stupid enough," one said. "What do you think?"

Beside him was a huge lever set into the ground and marked "Ye Sword Release Mechanism."

"Let's see how he shapes up," said the smallest wizard. "Can't be too careful!"

Kron gripped the sword and heaved. The crowd went silent. There was a long moment while the sword and Kron vibrated gently and he gasped for breath.

"Hard luck!" cried the old wizard. "Now for the next try!"

Alan crept into the tent and hid behind a table, while the three wizards watched Kron's second attempt at pulling the sword from the stone.

"Big, strong and stupid," one said. "I say, let him pull it out and he can become king and then he'll do what he's told, and we'll all be on the gravy train.'"

"Looks a bit willful," said the smallest wizard. "It's risky, the sword in the stone dodge. Look at old Merlin—thought he was made for life, next thing you know, the lad gets ideas of his own and starts spending money on Round Tables and stuff."

"Second try, sorry," said the wizard on the stage. "Let's give him a big hand, folks, and one more attempt."

Kron spat on his hands and grasped the sword for the third time . . .

"I dunno," said the smallest wizard. "Could be a troublemaker."

So was Alan. He ran forward and pulled the sword release lever. The crowd outside gasped. So did Kron. The sword began, very slowly, to rise.

The wizards looked around, shouted at Alan, and all three snatched the lever. The crowds gasped again. It looked as though the stone was pulling back.

Unfortunately for the wizards in the tent, they were not very well organized and got in each other's way. Alan managed to pull the lever again. Outside, the sword began to come out of the stone for the second time. Kron's knees were knocking with the effort.

Alan got a clip round the ear and the lever was pushed back. The sword sank once more.

Alan rolled under the tent flap and ran to the stone, with a couple of the wizards after him.

"I said it was a fix!" he yelled. "Kron, they're holding it down!"

"Well, folks, that's about enough for—" began the old wizard next to Kron, hurriedly.

Kron took one hand off the sword and pulled the wizard's pointy hat over his eyes. Then he gripped the sword again, shifted his feet, gritted his teeth, and tugged.

The sword rose. So did several yards of turf. There were horrible grinding noises underground, and various metal levers and cogwheels sailed into the air. The stone shattered, exposing a complicated arrangement of magnets. The sword was free.

"Okay," said Kron, advancing on the cowering wizards. "What about the cuddly toy?"

"And the key," said Alan. "Come on—where's the key?"

The smallest wizard gingerly handed Alan a large black key.

"And the cuddly toy," said Kron. "And the holiday in wherever it is, and double, thingy, glazing, for my windows!" He raised the sword threateningly.

"I think we'd better forget about that," said Alan. He wasn't sure how good swords were against magic, but the wizards were beginning to get over their shock and it was just possibly not a good idea to hang around.

Sure enough, the oldest wizard pulled his hat off, raised one hand, screamed a magic word, and sent a fireball hurtling towards them. Kron was so angry he wouldn't have ducked if Alan hadn't kicked his ankle.

There was a sudden whooshing noise and a broomstick hovered in the air next to them, with Grubble hanging on for dear life.

"Get on!" he shouted. "Come on, this isn't easy to control!"

"I won fair and square," said Kron. "I'm entitled!"

"You'll be entitled to being a frog if you hang around; this is heavy magic coming down here!" shouted Grubble.

Finally, Kron jumped on, with Alan hanging on to the bristles. Surprisingly, since it was one of the broomsticks Grubble sold, it didn't snap in half. Instead, it dipped slightly and then tore across the ground with the wizards sending fireballs after it.

People scattered out of the way, stalls were overturned, but finally the overloaded broom gained some height.

"Five keys!" yelled Grubble triumphantly above the rushing wind. "Hold tight—off we go!"

There was an explosion of rainbow light and the broomstick and its riders vanished.

The broomstick with Kron, Alan, and Grubble the Utterly Untrustworthy on board flew silently through a tunnel of weird flashing lights and colors.

"Where are we going, precisely?" said Kron.

Grubble didn't look round. "It remains to be seen," he said.

"You mean you don't know?" said Kron. "We're flying through all this—"

"Quite good special effects," put in Alan.

"Yeah, quite good special effects," added Kron, uncertainly, "and, like, you don't know where we're going to come out?"

"Not exactly *know*, since you put it like that," said the wizard wretchedly. "I more sort of guess."

"I ought to tie you in a knot," growled Kron.

"It's only my magic that's keeping us going," said the wizard. "Think you can fly this thing?"

"No."

"Well, shut up then."

The magic tunnel disappeared, and the broomstick swooped down over a desert landscape. Most of it was just sand, but there was a pyramid immediately below them. It was very big and incredibly old.

"The Great Pyramid of Zag," said Grubble, swooping down

low for a better look. "Very famous. One of the Nine Fairly Interesting Wonders of the World, you know."

"What were the others?" asked Kron.

"Oh, nothing much," said the wizard. "Hold tight, I'm going to try to land. Have you ever flown a broomstick, boy?"

"No," said Alan.

"What a coincidence, neither have I," said Grubble.

Fortunately, the sand was quite soft, which was just as well.

"Not bad, that," said Grubble. Kron shook the sand out of his ears.

The pyramid loomed in front of them. There was a big door, crusted with age and rust. But there was a keyhole.

"Well," said Grubble to Kron. "Here are the keys, and you've got the boy, so in you go, and I'll just sort of stay outside and, er, sort of protect your rear, so to speak. Ow!"

Kron had grabbed his ear. "No," he said. "You come inside too, sort of, so to speak."

"What is the treasure, exactly?" said Alan.

"The legend says the treasures are the most valuable things in the universe," said Grubble.

"Yes, but WHAT are they?" said Alan.

Grubble fished an ancient-looking book out of his robe.

"Here," he said, "read what it says yourself."

Alan gingerly opened the book. It was very old and full of fiddly little pictures instead of writing. The wizard's fingers pointed at a page.

"Well, there's a picture of a house, a sort of boat, a giraffe, a rabbit upside down, two half-moons, and a wobbly thing with a hole in it," Alan said. "So what?"

"Ah, but that's hiero-hero-hairogly— old picture writing," said Grubble. "It means 'And The Great Zag said, In My Pyramid are Many Treasures But You May Also Find the Most Valuable Things in the Universe, Honestly, No Kidding, I Really Mean It.' Amazing, isn't it?"

"Come on," said Kron. "Unlock this door, and let's get a crack at all this amazing treasure."

The first key did unlock the door, and with some effort Kron managed to open it. There was a long dry passage inside.

They came to two more doors, which Kron unlocked and pulled open.

Absolutely nothing happened. No great stone balls rolled down, no trapdoors opened, there was an amazing lack of poisoned arrows shooting out of the walls.

The next door had some picture writing engraved over the lock.

It read: "Small rabbit, twiddly thing, bent tree, duck with hat on, two horses on a sort of bicycle," which Grubble said meant: "Secret Treasures, Right This Way."

"Oh no," said Kron. "Everyone will laugh at me when they hear about this!"

Grubble the wizard unlocked the fourth door, which swung back slowly. It revealed a large stone room, with walls covered in picture writing. On a raised slab in the middle of the floor was . . .

"Treasure!" breathed Grubble. He rushed over to it and fumbled through the piles of sacks and boxes.

A deep voice from nowhere special said: "Will You Take This and Go, Or Will You Seek the Most Valuable Things in the Universe?"

"Who said that?" said Kron.

"It wasn't me," said Alan. "But we ought to go."

"Oh, we want the Most Valuable Things," said Grubble, filling his pockets with diamonds. "This is just small stuff."

The door slammed shut. It was a heavy, dull sort of slam, the sort of slam that is particularly unpleasant when you happen to remember that the key is in the lock ON THE OTHER SIDE.

Then someone started laughing. You probably know the sort of laugh. It came from everywhere.

"If You Want the Most Valuable Things in the Universe, You'd Better Start Looking," it boomed. "P.S., The Ceiling Is Coming Down."

"We'd better look for the secret door," said Alan. The others stared at him. "There's always a secret door," he pointed out.

He and the wizard started banging on the walls. Kron didn't—the ceiling was already just above his head. He spat on his hands and tried to hold it back.

"There's no secret door," wailed Grubble. "We're doomed!"

"Try some magic," said Alan.

"And hurry up!" muttered Kron, who was beginning to sag under the weight of the ceiling.

"I have! It won't work!"

There was a *crack*, and Kron disappeared. They crawled over to the spot where he had been—the ceiling was very low now—and saw him sitting in a tunnel some way below.

"You were standing on it all the time!" said Grubble accusingly. "Come on, give us a hand down!"

They hurried along the dark corridor, with Kron in the lead

and the wizard lagging behind because of all the treasure he had stuffed into his boots, his hat, and every pocket.

Suddenly Kron stopped and stared hard at the floor. Then he snatched one of the gold bars that Grubble was carrying and tossed it onto a slab a little way ahead.

There was a nasty metal noise and several rusty sword blades shot out of the wall.

"Nice chap, this Zag," said Kron, kicking the blades until they snapped. "Come on!"

Alan grabbed his belt.

"If I was Zag, I'd set another trap just here," he said. "People wouldn't be looking for it and would be caught."

"Good thinking," said Kron, and snatched another bar from the wizard. He dropped it onto the next stone.

A dozen ancient spears dropped out of the ceiling and shattered on the floor.

"This Zag character had a lot of imagination," said Kron bitterly, looking at the spears.

"We've still got to find the Most Valuable Things in the Universe," bleated the wizard Grubble. "Don't go dropping my—"

The rest of the sentence was lost to view as the slab he was standing on tipped up. There was a scream, and a distant splash.

"Can you swim?" Kron asked Alan.

"I've got a Grade Three badge."

"What does that mean?"

"It means yes."

They jumped after the wizard, and landed in deep cold water. There was a spluttering noise as Kron surfaced dragging an unconscious Grubble with him.

"It's all the treasure in his pockets . . . he sank like a stone," said Kron. "Can you see anywhere to get out? I've just bitten an alligator and I think it's gone to get its friends."

Alan found some slimy steps and they crawled out, onto a dark ledge just above the water. A pitch-black tunnel led upwards.

Kron held the wizard upside down to let the water run out. Jewels bounced all over the ledge . . . and most of them fell in the water. Then they started up the tunnel . . . lost, soaking wet, and not happy at all.

After a while the tunnel leveled off, and then started to go downhill again. Once or twice, Kron had to hack his way through thick tangles of spider web. Grubble woke up and started complaining about all the treasure they had taken out of his pockets to make him lighter to carry.

"We still haven't found this Most Precious Treasure that Zag kept going on about," he said. "Anyone seen anything that looks like it? It'll probably be gold. What's that rumbling?"

They looked around. Through the gloom they could just make out a big stone ball, completely filling the passage, rolling down towards them.

"Oh, not that old trick again," said Kron. "Come on, we're supposed to run."

"It's a dead end," said Alan. The ball was quite near now.

"Grubble!" they both yelled. "Do some MAGIC!"

The wizard said: "I'm not all that good at this," and stuck out a finger. Green light flashed from it, and there was a terrific explosion. Dust filled the air; there was sunlight shining out through a hole in the roof. The stone ball had vanished.

"Come on," shouted Kron, "we can climb up the rubble!"

In a few minutes they were standing on the desert sand, with the pyramid quite some way off.

"Sunlight, freedom and fresh air," said Kron. "Now that's what I call treasure—" He stopped, and stared at Grubble, who backed away.

"The Most Valuable Things in the Universe!" he snarled. "That's what Zag meant. You gave up all that treasure for fresh air, you toad."

Alan sniffed. "Worth it, though," he said.

"That's it, that's it!" said Grubble, hiding behind the boy. "Better out here than in those tunnels, eh?"

"Anyway, we didn't lose it all," said Alan. He fished in his pocket and brought out four huge diamonds.

The last thing that was heard, as the three disappeared arguing over the sand, was Grubble saying: "Of course we can share them out equally. There's two for you two and two for me, too . . ."

The Quest for The Quest for the Keys
Or
Sometimes It's Right To Be Wrong

by Pat and Jan Harkin

We live not far from Boston Spa, the site of the British Library's newspaper archive. Colin Smythe has occasionally asked us to try and track down some of Sir Terry's earlier pieces of journalism, either in the local papers or trade journals.

In early 2022, Colin was contacted by a fan of Sir Terry who was seeking information about a serial called "The Quest for the Keys." As a child the fan had cut the installments from the newspapers and they were mounted on wall displays. To Colin's surprise, he had no record of the story ever being published and was fascinated to see the clippings. Sadly, they had been trimmed in a fashion which removed all references to newspaper and date of publication, though it was thought to be "fifty years old." Colin approached us and we arranged to visit the archive.

We were unsure when the serial might have been published. It mentioned the city of Morpork, otherwise first seen (as Ankh-Morpork) in *The Color of Magic*, which was published in 1983. We thought it unlikely that Sir Terry would have reused the name after publication of the novel and we already had an estimate that the story was "fifty years old," which gave us a rough publication window of 1972 to 1984. We decided to start at 1972 and work forwards, going through four newspapers: the *Western Daily Press*, the *Bucks Free Press*, the *Midweek Free Press*, and the *Bath and West Evening Chronicle*. Starting in 1972 was, in terms of finding the story, undoubtedly the wrong choice. But as events played out, it was most assuredly the right one!

We had decided to collect more information than we probably needed, rather than under-collect and have to return to the archive. Sir Terry's stories in the *Western Daily Press* were published in a section called the Sunshine Club. Many authors wrote these serials. We collected the author's name, story title and date of publication for every issue so that we could be sure we hadn't left any gaps in the record. We worked individually and then, at the end of the afternoon, we combined our findings. At the beginning of February 2022, Jan read a list to me which included "The Blackbury Thing" and "Blackbury Weather," and noted the unusual spelling of "blackberry." That rang a bell for me, as many of Sir Terry's children's stories are set in Blackbury, and I was surprised to see the author listed as Patrick Kearns. I read the chapters and found that "Blackbury Weather" was set in "the little Gritshire market town of Blackbury." Looking back through the material we'd already cataloged revealed a further five stories by Kearns.

We sent photographs of the stories to Colin and were delighted when he confirmed our suspicion—these were previously unknown stories by Sir Terry! He also pointed out a further clue to the author's identity, in addition to the style of writing: Sir Terry's mother's maiden name was Kearns. Over the following weeks we found a few more Kearns tales but no other new pseudonyms. By mid-March we still hadn't found "The Quest for the Keys" but we did make another discovery.

From May 1, 1970, one of Sir Terry's stories—"Mr. Brown's Holiday Accident"—written under the already known pseudonym Uncle Jim, was serialized in five instalments in the *Bucks Free Press*. Unfortunately, it seemed that the final episode—for May 29—was never printed; that week's paper was affected by industrial action, and the British Newspaper Archive copy of the June 6 issue has the pencil annotation "May 29th NP." Although Colin had copies of parts one to four of the story, the conclusion was thought to be lost.

The *Bucks Free Press* did not assign titles to their stories and instead we used the names under which they appear on Colin's website. At the end of each day's work, we would use Colin's site to attach the "official" title to each piece. One evening I was doing this task and found that Colin's site said the issue I had on-screen was the lost issue! The date was correct, the newspaper was correct and the story mentioned Mr. Brown. A quick check with Colin confirmed this was the missing piece. It appears that the May 29, 1970, issue of the *Bucks Free Press* was never sold—it was given away with that day's *Midweek Free Press*. We're especially proud of that discovery (even though it is by far the smallest), as it contains a plot element next used in *Mort*, almost twenty years later.*

Eventually, we discovered "The Quest for the Keys" in the *Western Daily Press*. It was serialized in thirty-six installments,

---

* We'll leave it for you to find.

initially daily from July 30, 1984, then weekly from September 8, 1984. It also featured a competition—something not preserved in the clippings. Well done Kate Browning, Justin Whitfield, Sarah Arnot, and Angela Hooper. We hope you enjoyed your tents!

We went to Boston Spa sixteen times, spending roughly sixty hours poring over vast, heavy bound volumes of newspapers. This was far more than we would have done had we made the right decision at the start and worked backwards from the end of 1984. We would have found "The Quest for the Keys" almost immediately, possibly even in the very first week. But then we'd never have found the works of Patrick Kearns and "Mr. Brown's Holiday Accident" would have remained unfinished indefinitely.

I think we were right to be wrong.

Pat and Jan Harkin
February 2023

Arnold, the Bominable Snowman

"Granny Weatherwax was not lost. She wasn't the kind of person who ever became lost. It was just that, at the moment, while she knew exactly where SHE was, she didn't know the position of anywhere else." (Wyrd Sisters)

As it goes with witches so—it turns out—it sometimes happens with stories. A little while after pressing Ctrl-P on the hardcover of *A Stroke of the Pen*, a further tale was discovered stuffed down the back of Colin Smythe's* metaphorical sofa. The full text of "Arnold, The Bominable Snowman" has now been lovingly included for this new edition.

Rob Wilkins

* Sir Terry's agent and original publisher.

Once upon a time there was a snowman. He wasn't an abominable one, like the ones that grunt and sneeze up on distant Tibetan mountains, but quite English and completely bominable.

He was built by some children, but when everyone had gone to bed he jumped around the lawn and waved his arms to keep warm.

"Blow this for a lark," he said. "Those kids ought to know it takes more than a jumble sale hat and three bits of coal stuck down your tummy to keep you warm on frosty nights!"

There was a bang and a shower of sparks and a tall lady appeared as if by magic. She was wearing a very severe business suit and horn-rimmed glasses, and was peering at a list.

"I'm your fairy godmother," she said, uncertainly.

"I didn't know snowmen had fairy godmothers," said the snowman. You must admit it sounds a bit unlikely.

"I dunno," said the lady. "You're on my list. A. Snowman, it says here."

"That's A for Arnold," said Arnold Snowman.

"Well, Arnold, I'm empowered to grant you a wish under the Magic Wishes (Wishful Thinking) Act, Clause 19a. Be quick—I've got several other calls to make!"

Quick as a flash Arnold Snowman said: "I'd like a nice warm overcoat!"

Well, of course, he very nearly melted when he wore it. When his fairy godmother came back he was half his normal size.

So instead he asked for a nice warm fire.

That kept him warm too, but melted him just the same. In fact, if there hadn't been a power cut he'd have melted clean away.

"You're a pretty ignorant snowman, and snowmen aren't generally very brainy," said his fairy godmother. "You've got one last wish—and don't ask for something daft like a plateful of curry."

Soon the sun came up and a thaw set in, and at last Arnold Snowman burst out: "I want to be somewhere nice and cold!"

And who should be passing by but the manager of a frozen fish-fingers firm who saw that Arnold Snowman could keep cool in an emergency. He offered him a job on the spot as head packer in the very coldest of the frozen-fish warehouses, with good wages and the chance of promotion to Chief Breadcrumb Sprinkler.

And because Arnold Snowman was such a cool customer he soon made enough money to retire to a deckchair at the North Pole.

Moral: Electricity is clean, quick, efficient, and scarce. It's smart to be cool. And if you're a snowman you're bound to get on.

Text Acknowledgments

The publisher would like to thank Colin Smythe and Pat and Jan Harkin for providing the following source information.

All stories collected here were originally published in the *Western Daily Press*, either under Terry's own name or the pseudonym Patrick Kearns, or in the *Bucks Free Press*, under the pseudonym Uncle Jim, as indicated below.

How It All Began . . .
First published in the *Western Daily Press*, June 12, 16, 19, 1971, under the pseudonym Patrick Kearns.

The Fossil Beach
First published in the *Western Daily Press*, May 5, 9, 12, 16, 19, 23, 26; June 2, 6, 1973, under the pseudonym Patrick Kearns.

The Real Wild West
First published in the *Western Daily Press*, February 2, 5, 9, 12, 16, 19, 23, 1972, under the pseudonym Patrick Kearns.

How Scrooge Saw the Spectral Light (Ho! Ho! Ho!) and Went Happily Back to Humbug
First published in the *Western Daily Press*, December 24, 1975, under the pseudonym Patrick Kearns.

Wanted: A Fat, Jolly Man with a Red Woolly Hat
First published in the *Western Daily Press*, December 24, 1974, under the pseudonym Patrick Kearns.

A Partridge in a Post Box
First published in the *Western Daily Press*, December 24, 1970, under the pseudonym Patrick Kearns.

The New Father Christmas
First published in the *Western Daily Press*, December 23, 1972, under the pseudonym Patrick Kearns.

The Great Blackbury Pie
This version originally published in the *Western Daily Press*, November 18, 21, 1970, under Terry's own name. Reprinted in the *Western Daily Press*, under the title "The Great Pie of Blackbury," December 30, 1992.

This is a revised version of "The Blackbury Pie" which was first published in the *Bucks Free Press*, December 15, 22, 1967, under the pseudonym Uncle Jim. It was later revised again and included in the short story collection *Father Christmas's Fake Beard and Other Stories* (Doubleday, Random House Children's Publishers, 2017).

How Good King Wenceslas Went Pop for the DJ's Feast of Stephen
First published in the *Western Daily Press*, December 24, 1971, under the pseudonym Patrick Kearns.

Dragon Quest
This version originally published in the *Western Daily Press*, December 6, 9, 13, 16, 20, 27, 30, 1972, under the pseudonym Patrick Kearns.

This is a revised version of "Dragons at Crumbling Castle," which was first published in the *Bucks Free Press* in September 1966 under the pseudonym Uncle Jim. It was later revised again and included in the short story collection *Dragons at Crumbling Castle and Other Stories* (Doubleday, Random House Children's Publishers, 2014).

The Gnomes from Home
First published in the *Western Daily Press*, August 4, 7, 11, 14, 1971 under the pseudonym Patrick Kearns.

From the Horse's Mouth
This version published in the *Western Daily Press*, May 31; June 3, 7, 10, 14, 17, 1972 under the pseudonym Patrick Kearns.

This is a revised version of Terry's story "Johnno, The Talking Horse," which was first published in the *Bucks Free Press*, April 28; May 5, 12, 19, 25, 1972, under the pseudonym Uncle Jim. It was later revised and reprinted in the deluxe edition of *The Witch's Vacuum Cleaner and Other Stories* (Doubleday, Random House Children's Publishers, 2016) and in *The Time-Travelling Caveman and Other Stories* (Doubleday, Random House Children's Publishers, 2020).

Blackbury Weather
First published in the *Western Daily Press*, March 18, 22, 25, 29; April 1, 1972 under the pseudonym Patrick Kearns.

The Blackbury Jungle
First published in the *Bucks Free Press*, May 25; June 1, 8, 15, 22, 1973, under the pseudonym Uncle Jim.

The Haunted Steamroller

First published in the *Western Daily Press*, June 13, 16, 20, 23, 27, 30; July 4, 1973, under the pseudonym Patrick Kearns.

The Money Tree

First published in the *Western Daily Press*, August 18, 21, 22, 25, 28, 1971 under the pseudonym Patrick Kearns.

The Blackbury Thing

First published in the *Western Daily Press*, March 1, 4, 9, 11, 15, 1972 under the pseudonym Patrick Kearns.

Mr. Brown's Holiday Accident

First published in the *Bucks Free Press*, under the pseudonym Uncle Jim, May 1, 8, 15, 22, 1970; concluded in the *Bucks Free Press Midweek*, June 3.

Pilgarlic Towers

First published in the *Western Daily Press*, July 17, 21, 24, 29, 31, 1971 under the pseudonym Patrick Kearns.

The Quest for the Keys

First published in the *Western Daily Press*, July 30, 31; August 1, 2, 3, 4, 6, 7, 8, 9, 10, 11, 13, 14, 15, 16, 17, 18, 20, 21, 22, 23, 24, 25, 27, 28, 29, 30, 31; September 1, 8, 15, 22, 29; October 6, 13, 1984, under Terry's own name.

On August 6, the *Press* announced a competition to find the keys, clues being hidden in each episode of the following week.

Arnold, The Bominable Snowman

First published in the Western Daily Press, December 24, 1973, under the pseudonym Patrick Kearns.

* * * *

All interior story illustrations are by Andrew Davidson.

About the Author

Terry Pratchett (1948–2015) is the acclaimed creator of the globally revered Discworld series, the first of which, *The Color of Magic*, was published in 1983. In all, he authored more than fifty bestselling books, which have sold more than one hundred million copies worldwide. His novels have been widely adapted for stage and screen, and he was the winner of multiple prizes, including the Carnegie Medal. He was awarded a knighthood by Queen Elizabeth II for services to literature in 2009, although he always wryly maintained that his greatest service to literature was to avoid writing any.

TERRY PRATCHETT'S DISCWORLD

THE WIZARDS SERIES

"UNADULTERATED FUN." —*San Francisco Chronicle*

THE CITY WATCH SERIES

TERRY PRATCHETT'S DISCWORLD

THE WITCHES SERIES

THE ADVENTURES OF TIFFANY ACHING, WITCH-IN-TRAINING